MW01166997

Note for Librarians: A cataloguing record for this book is available from Library
and Archives Canada at www.collectionscanada.ca/amicus/index-e.html

ISBN 1-4120-9737-1

Printed in Victoria, BC, Canada. Printed on paper with minimum 30% recycled fibre.
Trafford's print shop runs on "green energy" from solar, wind and other environmentally-friendly
power sources.

TRAFFORD
PUBLISHING™

Offices in Canada, USA, Ireland and UK

Book sales for North America and international:
Trafford Publishing, 6E–2333 Government St.,
Victoria, BC V8T 4P4 CANADA
phone 250 383 6864 (toll-free 1 888 232 4444)
fax 250 383 6804; email to orders@trafford.com
Book sales in Europe:
Trafford Publishing (UK) Limited, 9 Park End Street, 2nd Floor
Oxford, UK OX1 1HH UNITED KINGDOM
phone +44 (0)1865 722 113 (local rate 0845 230 9601)
facsimile +44 (0)1865 722 868; info.uk@trafford.com
Order online at:
trafford.com/06-1493

10 9 8 7 6 5 4 3 2

The Fig Tree

By

Melody Kay Danals

This book is for all my family.

Jesus answered and said unto him, because I said unto thee, I saw thee under the fig tree, believest thou? Thou shalt see greater things than these.
John 1:50

But they shall sit every man under his vine and under his fig tree; and none shall make them afraid, for the mouth of the Lord of hosts hath spoken it.
Micah 4:4

In that day, saith the Lord of hosts, shall ye call every man his neighbor under the vine and under the fig tree.
Zechariah 3:10

And the stars of heaven fell unto the earth, even as a fig tree casteth her untimely figs, when she is shaken of a mighty wind.
Revelation 6:13

Acknowledgements

Thanks to all my children, Nathan and his wife Olga, Andrew and his new bride Anna, and Stephen. They have continued to back me in my writing. Thanks to my husband Ken for helping me put this book together.

To my parents Charlie and Eula Langford for their continued inspiration, and to my mother-in-law JoAnn Collins for editing this book.

Thanks to my sister Phyllis, her husband Gale and my brother Robbie for being such good witnesses for God in their daily life and having great children that have inspired me. I have used some of my nephew Jon's words in my book. His letter was written to me while he was on a mission trip to Africa.

Thanks to my friend Barbara Hester, who is always there to encourage me. Thank you to all my friends and family at Rehoboth Baptist Church.

Thanks to my Lilburn school family where I work as a parapro. They cheer me on daily to continue writing.

Chapter 1

1968

She was intensely watching the glowing light of the T.V. in front of her. Her mom was pacing behind the couch talking, but Tilly had long since tuned her out and the T.V. took total control of her attention. The popsicle Tilly was licking was getting all over her face and dripping on her already dirty shirt. The images flashing in front of her were the only interest the eight-year-old cared about. Her stringy blond hair fell into the red popsicle and she brushed it back getting her hand stuck in her hair. She jerked at it pulling her hair, but she did not take her hazel eyes off the T.V.

"Oh Tilly, you are getting popsicle all over the place. Go clean up now," her mom said and gave her a quick tap on the head as she continued to primp for her date. Tilly did not move, ignoring her mom was easy to do. All her mom cared about was the steady stream of men coming in and out. Her mom's name was Bonnie, or a least that is what she liked to be called. Tilly thought she knew her

4

mom's real name, but she didn't care to recall it.

"Now Tilly, be sure to get your brother and sister in the bed soon." Her mom was barking orders as she fluffed her hair to the highest peak. Tilly did not move off the couch. A car horn blew from outside and her mom gave herself one last glance in the mirror next to the door. She puffed her hair on each side and looked sideways. She shook her head, not quite satisfied, but the car horn blew again from outside.

"Oh all right, I'm coming! Tilly if you need anything, you call Miss June. I'm going. Hey, I said I was going!" Bonnie rolled her eyes and continued out the door and down the steps of the creaky porch. She paid no attention to the loose step because she knew how to step on it without throwing herself. Any unsuspecting soul, unfamiliar with the steps, often took a tumble. She got into the car and it sped away; and not much thought was given to the small frail girl inside.

Bonnie was young and pregnant when she got married. Marriages starting out as this one did often failed and hers failed miserably. She did not know where her ex-husband was. She had heard rumors that he was in jail, but she heard many things about him and did not care. Men were everything to her, and when she could find one to keep her up a while then that was fine. She worked odd jobs now and again, but she often got fired for not getting to work on time. She partied too much.

Tilly was often left to her own devices and with too much responsibility. She was in charge of her little sister of six and her brother of four. Mrs. Green's house next door was the only oasis Tilly had in the turbulent world around her. "Miss June," they called her. She was widowed and never had children of her own, but she felt she had raised hundreds in the years of her teaching career. Retired and lonely the pair found comfort in each other.

Still sitting on the couch, Tilly finished her popsicle. Anyone giving her a quick glance would know the flavor of popsicle she had just eaten. The possibility was strong that the signs of the red color would linger around her mouth even into the next day. The hot summer sun would only complete the picture after she ran and climbed trees, wiping her mouth with the Georgia red dirt. A bath to Tilly was nothing more then a dip in a tub that could have something growing in it. There was a knock at the door and Tilly finally turned away from the T.V. It was Miss June. Tilly then heard Bobby crying.

"Is everything all right?" Miss June was asking as she put her hand up to the holey, rusty screen door and pulled it open. It squeaked as it opened. Miss June had grown accustomed to the odd house and never stumbled again on the steps after the first fall. When she entered the house, she heard yelling.

"Sis hit me!" Bobby cried.

"You are a big baby!" Sis yelled back.

"Stop it you two. Why did you hit Bobby?" Tilly had had it with these two. They bickered all the time. She just wanted to watch her show.

"He won't stop following me. Make him stop!" Sis was whining and Tilly hated that. She took Bobby by the hand and led him to the couch.

"You can watch T.V. with me. You have to stop crying though," Tilly said. She looked up to see Miss June puttering around in the kitchen.

"Hey, Miss June! Mom's gone again." Tilly sort of thought Miss June knew that because she showed up a lot after her mom left.

"I had all this chicken left after I cooked today and I thought, well I can't just toss it out so I brought it to you." She was clearing a place on the table, but it proved to be difficult. She then had to find something to clean the table with. She bit back the words she would like to say.

"Why don't you kids go wash up while I put out this food," Miss June said as she worked. She did not have to tell them twice before they scampered toward the bathroom, pushing each other as they went down the hall. They all tried to get into the bathroom doorway at once. When they pushed through they all plopped on the floor. Bobby took the tub and the girls fought over the sink. Miss June just shook her head as she cleaned the kitchen. She couldn't do too much or Bonnie would get snippy with her. When Bonnie felt threatened she was like a cat about to pounce.

The children finished their food with lightning speed and Miss June gave them a hug. She got rid of the "evidence" that would give away the fact that she had fed the kids, and said "bye" to them. When she had hurdled the steps she turned around and yelled back, "Tilly, don't forget to ask your mom about Vacation Bible School. It starts next week!" Even before she reached her front door, she thought she had already figured what Bonnie would say. She would let them go; after all it was free babysitting for a week. She shook her head as she went into her house.

Tilly was asleep on the couch when her mom and the "man-friend" arrived, banging the door loudly and laughing. Bonnie plopped on the couch right on top of Tilly. Tilly made a sound.

"Oh, Tilly, I did not see you there." Bonnie hiccupped the words and laughed. "Why are you still up? Get to bed!" She took Tilly's arm roughly, slung her toward the hall and gave her backside a kick. She again shrilled with drunken laughter. Tilly turned around rubbing her backside just in time to see her mother fall into the arms of the equally drunken man. They swaggered around the room as if in a dance hall singing to music that only existed in their minds. They would not remember much the next morning. Tilly was staring when her mom caught her eye. The look said it all. The man was watching them.

"Sorry Joe, kids ya know," Bonnie said.

Tilly was in her room, tears streaming down her face. She had waited up for her mom because it was after midnight and it was her birthday. She had visions of greeting her mom and having her sing "Happy Birthday" to her in her high pitched out-of-tune voice. After that they would have danced around the room, but instead her mom was dancing with a stranger. Her mom would not remember now, because she would sleep all day tomorrow and get up late and be "cranky." Maybe Miss June remembered. She tried to think happy thoughts, and Vacation Bible School sounded like a good thing to look forward to.

Tilly woke up the next day and hurried to the mirror. She looked at herself sideways and poked out her chest. She slowly deflated. Nothing! When would she look like her friend Fran? Fran was eleven and wore a real bra. She wanted one too. She was looking intently at the image in front of her as if in hope of a change. She made faces at herself.

"What ya doing?" It was Bobby.

"Bobby, go away. Don't sneak up on people!" Tilly snapped.

"But I'm hungry," Bobby whined.

"Ok, I'm coming," Tilly said and started toward the kitchen. Bobby got out the milk. Sis came in with her nose wrinkled. "What is that awful smell?" she asked. Tilly turned around and took the milk from Bobby. They all bent over the cereal he had poured the milk on and gagged.

"Bobby, go to Miss June's and get some milk," Tilly ordered. Bobby scampered out and was careful not to bang the screen door. All the children knew not to wake their mom.

They had had too many bad experiences when that happened.

"Hey kids!" A voice came from behind Sis and Tilly. They slowly turned around. It was mom's "friend." He stood yawning and scratching his bald head. He gave them a piercing look from his dark eyes.

"Sis, go wash your hands," Tilly said. Sis was about to argue, but Tilly gave her a look. Sis passed the man, looking him over. He rushed at her and yelled, "Boo!" Sis screeched and ran down the hall. Tilly was still staring at the man. He walked over and took the milk from her hand. Before Tilly could say anything, he took a big swig and promptly spewed it out in the sink. Tilly bit her lip to keep from laughing.

"Ya little brat! Why didn't you tell me?" He swung around and Tilly just missed the back of his hand when she ducked.

"Hey, a body is trying to sleep. What is all the noise?" Bonnie was in the kitchen, her hair looked like she had stuck her finger into an electrical outlet. Her make-up was smeared all over her face. She was a mess.

"Ya brat here tried to poison me," Joe said.

"I did not, you are just stupid enough to drink sour milk," said Tilly. Her temper was showing and she was ready for a showdown. Bonnie walked over and slapped her.

11

"You apologize now you smart-mouthed ungrateful little..." Bonnie stopped yelling when Bobby burst into the room slamming the door. She held her head and groaned. She turned to Joe and told him to go home. Joe gathered up his stuff, and turned around before he continued out the door.

"I'll see ya next Friday uh?" Bonnie just gave a wave and went to her bedroom. Tilly knew she would sleep the rest of the day. She hoped she would anyway. Tilly hoped she would have a better life, better than her mom had offered her. She thought there would have to be a place in this world for her. She cleaned up, dreaming about the future.

Tilly heard Miss June's car horn blow on that long awaited day for Vacation Bible School. It was something different and somewhere else to go. This week she was going to go everyday somewhere besides this house of turmoil, and the pressure would be off her for a while. Taking care of everyone was a challenge. She saw that Bobby was eating a sticky bun and that Sis was shoeless. The car horn blew again, and Tilly raced to retrieve a pair of red tennis shoes for Sis and grabbed a towel to wash Bobbie's face. Tilly looked at herself in the mirror on the wall and declared herself ready. She gathered Sis and

Bobby and almost ran into Miss June on the porch.

"Oh there you are. Are you ready?" Miss June asked. Tilly missed the look Miss June had on her face. Miss June observed Bobby's plaid shorts and striped shirt. His sandals were flopping on his feet. They must have been hand-me-downs. As she opened the car door she saw the torn lace on the collar of the dirty little yellow dress Sis had on. Her little red tennis shoes topped off the outfit. When she got behind the wheel Tilly was sitting in the front. Tilly had made some attempt to look nice, but the dress was too small. She had on her dime store flip flops with the plastic flowers attached on top. Her painted toes and fingernails were chipped, and she forgot to comb the back of her hair. Miss June hoped Christian love would overlook those faults at church, but she knew some church members could be cruel. These kids would not understand that many call themselves Christians, but there were very few true Christians in the world.

They rolled up to the small church. Tilly looked up at the steeple against the blue sky. For Tilly that moment in time would always stay with her. The steeple of a church against a beautiful sky would always bring comfort to her. She would probably never know why, since that is how life goes. Small moments in life make the larger picture.

The kids were all running around outside on the steps and playing tag. Tilly had an overwhelming urge to join them in their merriment. She held back because Bobby was clinging to her and Sis looked scared.

"We need to get you in the right line to march in." Miss June was trying to guide the kids over to the others, and tried to ease them in by calling some of the other children over to meet them. They got in line and marched in to the tune of a nice song played on the piano.

Inside the church Tilly heard about God's love. She was listening intensely and hoping she could understand that kind of love. It would be many years before Tilly recalled these summers she spent in the church during Vacation Bible School. She enjoyed the clay print hands they made. She would remember the kool-aid and the cookies she stuck her finger through as she bit around the edges, and laughed with her new friends. Tilly would often draw on the truths she learned during these precious years in the summers of Vacation Bible School. She learned of God's unconditional love.

On the way home Tilly was quiet. Miss June did not try to bring her out of her silence. She knew Tilly well enough to know that she did not want to go back home and face what she had to face. Too much was on her little shoulders at home. Miss June could only help so much. They pulled up to the driveway. Bobby jumped out and raced in followed by Sis. Tilly got out slowly and shut the door.

"Bye Miss June, see ya tomorrow." Tilly shut the door and waved as the car pulled away.

Summer languished on. The songs of the bugs and other creatures sounded in the hot heat as if in chorus. Tilly was rocking on the front porch one afternoon. In her mind she had escaped to another place. Today she was a princess awaiting her prince. Would he come for her? She liked to read about such stories. The books took her to many places. She did not have a place to read in complete peace. Everyone wanted her for something. Her mom was the most needy. The last man had not come back and Bonnie was in deep depression. She was not working again, and Tilly was working odd jobs for the neighbors just to have money for food. Tilly could not wait for school to start. This was the first year she really wanted to go back to school. She could at least be a kid at school. Tilly dreamed of school and of maybe having a nice teacher that smelled good. Teachers always seem to smell good. Tilly pondered that for a

moment.   She continued her journey into
another world in her mind and listened to the
symphony of the southern summer sounds as
the day started to give way to the evening.
Soon she would see the lightning bugs
attempt to give light to the dark of the night.
She looked at the fig tree she and Miss June
had planted several years earlier as a project.
Its leaves were blowing in the night wind of
the coming storm.

Tilly took in things around her more than
most her age. She hugged herself as a slight
chill shrouded the night air. Wind was still
kicking up and a storm was coming fast. Tilly
sat there hugging herself as if hugging the
peace she found at that moment. Tilly would
not have too much peace in her life.

TRAFFORD
PUBLISHING™

Trafford Publishing
Suite 6E – 2333 Government Street Victoria BC V8T 4P4 Canada
Phone 250-383-6864 • Fax 250-383-6804
Toll-free 1-888-232-4444 (Canada & USA only)
www.trafford.com • orders@trafford.com

Trafford Publishing (UK) Ltd.
9 Park End Street, 2nd floor, Oxford, UK OX1 1HH
Local rate call 0845 230 9601   or   44 (0)1865 722 113
fax 44 (0)1865 722 868
info.UK@trafford.com

The Fig Tree

by Melody Kay Danals

ISBN 1-4120-9737-1

Available online:
trafford.com/06-1493

Tilly had a hard life growing
up with a drinking mom and a
revolving door of men in and out.
Tilly had to have faith in God to
survive.

TRAFFORD
PUBLISHING™

Chapter 2

1972

Tilly looked at herself in the mirror and made a face. She was twelve and she should look twelve, instead she looked, at best, ten. Her blond curls fell across her face and her hazel eyes stared back at her as she pushed her hair back. She would appreciate her young looks years from now, but right now it was lost on her. She liked boys, but they treated her as one of their buddies. She would take that much for right now. She was hoping she would turn into that swan one day. That had been a favorite story when she was younger. Tilly wanted to think and dream that she would be beautiful one day.

"Hey Tilly, are you going with me or not?" It was her friend Kate yelling from the front porch. Tilly quickly scooped up her much-earned money off the dresser and took off toward the front door. She bumped into Sis down the hall.

"Where ya going?" Sis asked as she shoved Tilly.

Tilly resisted the urge to blow her off without explanation   She felt sorry that she was leaving Sis in charge of Bobby.

"I'm going to a movie. If you need anything..."

"I know, I know. Go to Miss June's," Sis said finishing her sister's sentence. Again, Tilly felt a pang of guilt. Her mom had not come home from last night's date. If her mom had not been doing that a lot lately, she would worry, but she stopped worrying a long time ago.

"Tilly if ya don't hurry, we will miss the movie!" Kate was yelling.

"I'm coming!" Tilly yelled back.

Tilly glanced back at Sis in time to see her mocking Kate. She had her hands on her hips mouthing the words Kate had yelled. Tilly gave her a pop on the arm and ran to the door with Sis on her heels. Tilly grabbed Kate by the arm and took off down the steps to get away, forgetting about the loose step. Both girls took a tumble down the steps and got up laughing.

"That's what you get!" Sis had witnessed the fall and could hardly get the words out, she was laughing so hard. Tilly and Kate skipped back to Kate's house, and her big brother drove them to the movie theater.

Tilly watched the movie with intense interest in the leading man. He was blond and had blue eyes the color that she had only seen in the sky. She was in love for the first time. Her heart pounded as he fought off the bad guys. Tilly was eating a candy bar and when the most wonderful man she had ever seen kissed the lady on screen, she bit so hard on the candy bar, it fell on her lap in pieces.

"Hey, you were going to share that candy bar." Kate was more worried about the candy bar than any man in the movie. Tilly did not respond. Kate continued to protest the loss of the candy bar amidst sounds from the people around shushing her. Tilly did not care. When the movie was over, Tilly walked out of the theater as if in a dream. Kate was yapping away about something.

"Are you listening?" Kate shook Tilly.

"What?" Tilly was coming back to earth.

"Well, what is wrong with you?" Kate snapped.

"Wasn't he the most wonderful man on earth?" Tilly asked dreamily.

"Who?" Kate was looking around.

"Tim," Tilly said as if she had actually known him.

"Tim who?" Kate still looked bewildered.

"You know, in the movie." Tilly could not believe Kate did not notice the most beautiful blue eyes she had ever seen.

"Tilly, he is too old for you," Kate said rolling her eyes and tossing her bright red hair.

"He is not," Tilly protested.

"Well you will never know since you will never meet him," Kate said.

"You never know," Tilly answered back quickly.

"Oh Tilly, you are such a dreamer. You need to get real. Let's go to the ice cream shop." Kate was already forgetting the movie she had just seen and was ready for something else. Tilly, however, felt changed by the whole experience. Tilly would always have a soft heart for blond hair and blue-eyed boys, and she would never forget the man on the screen. She went to every movie he was in.

She arrived home and back to reality quickly enough. Her mom was home and in a mess. Bonnie stayed drunk almost all the time. Tilly took care of her as much as she could, but Bonnie would not get help. When they tried to get her help, she would not help herself. She continued to go downhill. Tilly watched her mom grab a glass and get some water. She could barely hold the glass.

"Where have ya been? Ya been with a boy?" Bonnie was slurring the questions.

"No, I went to the movie."

"Yeah, right."

"Why don't you believe me? I've done nothing wrong, unlike you!" Tilly was mad at her mom. She had already had enough.

"Do ya wan me ta get the belt? Ya don't talk ta me like that." Bonnie started after her, but Tilly ran to her room and shut the door. She leaned on the door and slid down on the floor weeping. She wanted to run away, but she stayed for Sis and Bobby.

At school Tilly started to fall behind. She wanted to fit in. Tilly did not care to be popular; she found her own group of friends and was satisfied. This group of friends, however, cared less about school work and more about the cigarette breaks in the bathroom. Tilly took to that vice like a duck to water. Tilly would soon be thirteen and she was at the age to try it all. It was on a day so typical as to almost be boring when things took a bad turn for Tilly at school. It would be the beginning of a series of problems in the future.

"Tilly Morgan!" Tilly jumped and dropped the cigarette she was puffing on. She closed her eyes and to herself said, "Oh no." With that she turned around to face Mrs. Gordon.

"Young lady come with me. I think a call home will be necessary." Mrs. Gordon continued to lecture her on the way to the office, but Tilly had a half smile on her face. Mrs. Gordon stopped suddenly and looked at Tilly.

"Do you think this is funny?" Mrs. Gordon asked.

"Oh no Mrs. Gordon," Tilly answered, but she did find it funny. She doubted her mom would answer the phone.

Tilly never got in trouble for that or anything she did in school. She was never praised for what she did good or admonished for what she did wrong by her mom as far as school was concerned. She was left to her own devices most of the time. Her mom wanted to live and let live. She cared whether Tilly was there for the other kids and that was it. Tilly continued down a path of badly chosen friends and poor choices. She became carefree about things; after all what difference did it make.

Chapter 3

Early 1976

Turning sixteen would mean more freedom than Tilly had ever had before. She could not wait until summer. Freedom, for whatever it was worth, to ride around at all hours with her friends in the ragged car her mom owned. Her mom stayed in most of the time, out of it and drunk. Sis was turning fourteen and Bobby was turning twelve. They did not need Tilly as much. They had all managed to stay in school. Tilly was already starting to skip school. She often found herself sneaking out. At first it was to go for a smoke with friends, but the door of the school became a revolving door for Tilly. Soon the teachers were concerned. They knew talking to the mom would make no difference, so they appealed to Tilly. Tilly was smart and could pass all the tests when she put her mind to it, but she wasn't interested. She barely got by.

"Mom, do we have to go to the family reunion? They all hate us," Tilly whined one day late in spring.

"Tilly, you know Aunt Bess expects us. She always gives us money." Bonnie was puttering around and in a rare sober state. Tilly rolled her eyes. Her mom made a point of going to the yearly family reunion. Aunt Bess always had a soft heart for Bonnie. She had helped raise her and felt responsible for her. She would slip a handful of bills in Bonnie's hand, maybe to alleviate some of her guilt. Who knows? Tilly just knew she did not like to go. Most of the relatives were not nice to them.

They pulled up to the old schoolhouse on Spring Road that had been the family gathering place for years. It, of course, was not used as a schoolhouse anymore. The car coughed itself out when it was turned off. Tilly sat staring out of the window. Bobby took off to join the softball game. Sis got out slowly, arms folded. Sis did not like this any better than Tilly. Bonnie got out and walked tippy toe in the just-rained-on ground. Stepping lightly, Bonnie had her hands up until she reached the back door. She retrieved the burnt casserole out of the back seat where Bobby had abandoned it. He had kept it in his lap the whole way.

"Mom, do we have to take that in?" Tilly said looking at the casserole with disgust.

"Tilly, you know it is proper to bring something. Besides if you had cooked something like I asked you, I would not have been rushed and burned this. I don't know what to make of you these days," Bonnie said and continued to walk toward the building.

"Come on girls." Bonnie was looking back and nodding toward the school house. The girls walked slowly behind Bonnie. A ball rolled over and hit Tilly in the leg. Picking up the ball she was going to throw it back, but cousin Jake came up to get it.

"Hey Tilly, ya'll jus gettin here?" Jake asked with an amused look on his face.

He understood Tilly. He had about the same upbringing. Tilly gave him her winning smile while brushing back a wayward curl.

"Yeah, we had to come," Tilly confided in a low voice. She was happy to see a kindred spirit. This might not be so bad.

Tilly pounced out of the old schoolhouse like a cat skirting out of a yard full of dogs. The old porch creaked when Tilly leaped on it and skirted out the door. Tilly looked back at the porch where a few people were sitting. She was glad to be outside. She had made the usual greetings and fake smiles, and listened to the droning of complaints about the aches and pains that overtook their aging bodies. Tilly would have thought Aunt Bertie's family would have been wiped out by now. They had diseases that nobody had heard of, and lived to complain year after year. They all seemed fit as a fiddle to Tilly and she lost patience with people who complained. Tilly knew another unknown illness would befall them for next year. Tilly thought that if something real really came upon the family, Aunt Bertie would just drop dead on the spot. Tilly was deep in thought when she spotted an old barn in the distance. Something lured her toward it. She walked through the uncut knee-high wet grass. It had recently rained and the damp grass slapped her bare legs. She felt the cold moisture seep into her sandals as she walked. Tilly didn't care and was intent on her target. She smelled the smoke before she saw it. She got closer to the open door.

The dilapidated old barn told a tale of a long life, not unlike a lot of aged barns scattered across the Georgia terrain, only a few hours from the hustle and bustle of Atlanta. This barn gave hints of a once thriving farm full of life. Tilly swiped at the insects buzzing around her head. She again smelled the familiar smells of home - alcohol and cigarettes. She crept closer to the wide opening. She was not surprised to see Jake. He looked up as if he had expected her.

"Come on in and join the party," Jake said and raised his beer.

Tilly, always admiring this cousin, took the can of beer that was beside him. He reached in his pocket and got a cigarette. She took it. He helped her light it. She puffed on it.

"Since when did you grow up?" Jake asked.

She took a swig of beer as if to make a point. She coughed and made a face.

"This is ya first beer. Well, well, leave it to me to corrupt you." Jake took the beer out of her hand. "Can't go back in there drunk and smelling of beer. This will have to wait."

Jake reached for her cigarette, but Tilly would not give that up. "Do you think I'm a baby?" She took another puff in defiance. Jake looked on in amusement.

"What brought ya out here?" Jake asked.

Tilly just looked at him and rolled her eyes. They both laughed.

"Ya mom getting money again?" Jake asked, and Tilly looked at him in surprise.

"Everybody knows," Jake continued.

Tilly felt small as she sat there contemplating.

"Don't worry we all have our problems," Jake said after a long silence.

Tilly took another puff on her cigarette. Jake got up and walked to the door.

"So why are you out here? Don't you want to eat?" Tilly was still sitting down.

Jake shrugged and blew out some smoke.

"You seem quiet today. You usually are telling jokes and making fun of everyone." Tilly was hoping to find out what dark cloud was hanging over her cousin.

"Did you see David?" Jake asked still not turning around.

"Yeah, he came back from Vietnam with nothing left of him. It is sad," Tilly replied.

They were discussing their cousin David who came back from the fields of Vietnam a couple of years before, crippled and with mental problems.

"I tried to talk to him, but he is not right in the head either. I hope I don't come back like that if there is another war."

Tilly jumped up. "Oh, you're not going in the army are you?"

"Yes, I decided to join up, honey." Jake turned around with despair in his face.

"You have to go then?" Tilly said. "Can't you get out of it?"

"No, it is too late, there is no place for the poor and the stupid like me. I quit school anyway and the war is over now. I can get an education in the army now," Jake said. He walked back and sat down on a bale of hay, rubbing his hand through his hair.

Tilly stood looking down at him. She knew going to Vietnam had been a death sentence. How many had died? The images of the pictures on T.V. passed before her. Many southern men went to war, and too many that she knew. She was thinking of the riots on the streets and the body bags. She was glad the war was over. As she was looking out of the barn door a pebble hit her foot. She stomped out the door.

"Bobby and Sis are you out there?" she said as she heard giggling.

"Ya'll get out of here now!" Tilly was yelling, and she heard more giggling and running about in the trees.

"We're gonna tell...we're gonna tell," chanted the children. "Tilly is smoking and we're gonna tell; and ya bottom gonna smoke..."

"Shut up ya'll or I'm gonna skin ya alive. Get!" Tilly was yelling and Jake came from behind her. "No ya won't, cause they won't live long enough!" With that Jake picked up a few pine cones and started throwing them toward the trees. There was more scampering and giggling and then silence.

"They will tell," Tilly said matter-of-factly.

"So, let them. What can your mother say?" Jake said as if he had plenty of experience in this area. He was right, her mother couldn't say anything to her and she would remind her. The ride home would not be fun, but she braced herself and determined to be strong.

"Let's go eat," Jake said and they walked toward the school house. They passed David in his wheelchair and Tilly felt a lump in her throat. She greeted David, and his mom looked up. "You remember Tilly, David?" There was no response and his mom kept rubbing his arm. Tilly bit her lip and went on past. Jake had not stopped and she understood. She caught up with him and went into the big room with all the long tables of food. She saw her mom's face, and it was clear Sis and Bobby had made good on their word. Sis smugly walked past Tilly and brushed her with her elbow.

"Ya gonna git it now," Sis said. Tilly shot her a look and hit at her but Sis barely missed the wound Tilly meant for her. Bobby wasn't worth going after.

"Don't worry, stand your ground." It was Jake behind her. He had a plate of food and had witnessed the whole scene. She turned around to get some food, careful to avoid her mother and stay close to Jake.

The tables were laden with fried chicken, potato salad, ambrosia, black-eyed peas, green beans and pies of all sorts. Tilly had to admit to being hungry, and grabbed a plate. Her mother was giving her cold stares as she dipped her food. Let her stare, she was going to do as Jake said and hold her ground. She felt somewhat stronger and decided to be more like Jake. Her mother had no right to say anything to her and she would let her know it.

She wasn't sure her strength would last beyond this moment, and when Jake wasn't beside her.

"Well young lady, what have you got to say for yourself?" Bonnie slammed the driver's side door as she got behind the wheel. Tilly had bravely sat up front. Tilly had dreaded this moment for two hours.

"Tilly was smoking! Tilly was smoking!" The chanting had begun in the back seat. Tilly got on her knees, and turning around on the seat started swiping at the two tormenters.

"Hey, sit down now, Tilly!" Bonnie popped Tilly on the bottom, grabbed her shirt and pulled her down. Tilly shook her mother away.

"What kind of attitude do you have? You need to be careful and not grow up too fast. Don't think I don't know about you smoking at school. They call. I'm just telling you now you need to straighten up," Bonnie said firmly.

Tilly sat staring at her mother as if she was looking at an alien. She heard something in her mom's voice she had never heard before. It was called caring, but Tilly's young mind wasn't going to allow her guard to go down.

"You don't have a right to say anything to me." Tilly crossed her arms.

"You watch your mouth," Bonnie said.

Silence hung in the car like a dark cloud on a summer day. Tilly couldn't resist the droning of the car and soon fell asleep. When they got home nothing more was said. Tilly knew Bonnie did not want to worry over her for long.

Chapter 4

Summer 1976

Tilly knew her mom was up to something, because she had not bothered Tilly about the reunion again. That was all right with Tilly, but she had no idea what would be occupying her mother. Tilly liked the peace and decided to push her luck by telling her mom about a job. She had approached Billy about working for him. Billy's was a small café at the edge of town. Everyone ate there once in a while. Tilly wanted some independence and decided that this was a good first step. Billy had known Tilly all of her life and was impressed with her. He gave her a job right away.

Bonnie took the news really well, but Tilly soon learned why. A new man was in her life and he was moving in. Tilly knew he was probably a creep before she met him. Well, with her new job and school, she would not worry about dealing with them. She only worried about Sis and Bobby. For herself, she had plans for the future - to work for a car and finish school.

A few days later Tilly was on her way out the door, ready for her first day at work. School would be starting soon and she would be working after school as well. She was contemplating this while she was walking out onto the porch. The screen gave the usual creaky sound and Tilly looked down at her watch to check the time. Tilly was startled by a yell from a male voice. After a string of obscenities came forth, Tilly stood a moment observing the man sprawled out on the ground. He was picking himself up and gathering his boxes from around him cursing the loose step that had thrown him. Tilly laughed to herself, but went to help him.

"I can handle this, but that step has got to be fixed. You must be Tilly. I heard a lot about you. I met Sis and Bobby, but you were never around when I picked up ya mom."

Tilly rolled her eyes and nodded. She mumbled some greeting and proceeded past him.

"Don't you even want to know my name?" asked the man, getting a little disgruntled. Tilly turned slowly and put her finger to her cheek as if to contemplate.

"Let's see, you could be Tom, Dick or Harry or…"

"Now see here missy, I'll have no disrespect from you. You are starting on the wrong foot with me already." The man was turning red with anger. His white sleeveless shirt hung over his big belly and poked out over the belt. He was middle-aged and had a rough face.

"Boy, mom can sure pick um..." With that Tilly walked toward her mom's car. She felt the man's eyes on her. She did not care. He was the same type of creature her mom had brought home numerous times. He was probably addicted to something, out of a job, no real home, and stupid. She would pretend he didn't exist. She, herself, would pick a good man - an important man with class - when she settled down. Tilly walked by the fig tree to check for figs then she passed by the magnolia trees and took a deep breath. This was a favorite scent to Tilly. She liked to pick the big flowers and float them in a bowl in her room. She walked over and picked up a large bloom on the sidewalk. She had to knock the ants off. She smelled it and put it to her cheek. She got into the car and put the flower beside her. She thought about what it would be like to fall in love. Tilly was at that age. She realized the time and quickly took off with the music blasting out as she sang to the song on the radio. She entered Billy's in a huff. Billy greeted her with a broom.

"See here, slow down, no fire here," Billy said.

"Don't I get to wait tables?" Tilly took the broom as if it were a bad date.

"Well no, you have to learn everything else first," Billy replied.

"Please…" Tilly pleaded.

"Now girl, I didn't give you that broom to dance a jig with, Get busy," Billy said sternly.

He knew he had his hands full with that one. He thought Tilly would be a good worker, so he did not mind.

A girl stood behind the counter surveying the scene before her. Tilly caught the dark eyes on her and immediately knew she had a friend. The girl gave her a wink.

"Hi, I'm Diane. Don't worry about waiting tables, it ain't special. It's hard work." Diane continued to size up the petite figure in front of her. She wasn't jealous because she felt a kindred spirit. 'You are going to stir up the boys around here." Diane was amused because this girl seemed to have no knowledge of her own beauty. During the summer Tilly had blossomed, but was unaware of it. Tilly had equal thoughts of Diane, she thought her to be attractive with her dark hair and eyes. She was older by a few years, but Tilly knew they could be friends.

"Get rid of the gum!" It was Billy who was barking orders. "And get to work, both of you." Tilly looked around and swallowed the gum. Diane rolled her eyes and said, "He is not so bad. His bark is worse than his bite. His son died in Vietnam and he has a daughter in school.   She ain't no angel right now and he worries over her."

Tilly started sweeping.   It was between the breakfast and lunch crowd, so she was able to sweep the whole place and clean up in the back some. Tilly took some trash out the back door and was dumping it. Diane was on break and was leaning up against the wall smoking.

"You still in school?" Diane took a puff of cigarette and was looking down at Tilly as she was dumping the trash.   Tilly pushed the trash down with her foot and said,

"Yeah, I will be a junior this year." Diane continued to stare at the girl and replied,

"I quit," and she kicked at a pebble.

"I plan to finish and get my own car," Tilly said.

"What will you do after that?" Diane asked. Tilly just shrugged her shoulders. She had not thought much beyond that.

"Do you have a boyfriend?" Diane continued to question Tilly.

"No, I don't date much."

"A pretty girl like you not dating?" Diane stated. Tilly grabbed her stray strand of hair and pushed it back.   She tried to remember when someone had actually called her pretty. Diane continued to talk about her engagement and her future plans, but it was lost on Tilly. They both went in to finish the lunch-hour crowd, and Tilly finished the day with very sore feet.

Tilly arrived home to a hub of activity. The music from the radio could be heard from the drive, and when Tilly opened the door the T.V. was blasting.

"Bobby, Sis, where are you?" Tilly turned off everything and looked around. She heard her mom laughing in the back yard.

"Hey, turn the T.V. back on!" It was Sis yelling from the kitchen.

"Where is Bobby?" Tilly asked her sister.

"I don't know, around somewhere." Sis was biting into a sandwich she had just made.

"Is that all you've had to eat for supper?" Tilly was looking at the sandwich. Sis gave her a look and plopped on the sofa. Tilly went to her room and looked out the window. Her mom and the new man were having drinks on the small back patio. Tilly shook her head and fell exhausted on the bed.

Tilly woke up the next morning with the sun in her eyes. Blinking her eyes and trying to adjust to her surroundings, she quickly closed the blinds. She looked over at the time and realized she had slept all night in her clothes. She had thirty minutes before she needed to be back at work. Tilly grabbed up some clean clothes and headed to the bathroom down the hall. She ran into the man who was coming out of the bathroom.

"Carl is my name missy, in case you want to know."

"Missy is not my name, in case you want to know." With that Tilly swept past him and slammed the door. Carl banged the door with his fist. It startled Tilly. She would have to keep a low profile with this one.

Tilly flung herself in the door of the café and Billy looked up but did not stop what he was doing. Tilly looked around and did not see Diane. She knew Diane lived in the small apartment above the store. Billy had been happy to let Diane use the place since she had nowhere else to call home. She had had a hard life, which is a big reason the girls would be drawn together. Diane came down a few minutes later, and Tilly wondered if that was the way it was here. Billy didn't seem to mind the lateness of either girl.

The days continued pretty much the same for the rest of the summer. Tilly spent some time with Miss June. Miss June taught her how to preserve figs. She also gave her some gardening lessons.

Tilly did not look forward to school as much as before, because she found satisfaction in a good hard day at work. She thought about quitting school, but when she threw the idea out at Billy he quickly set her straight.

Chapter 5

1976 -78

Looking across the campus of the high school, one would have a hard time telling one child from another. Long hair, bell bottom jeans, platform shoes and mini skirts all in a flurry of the first days of school after a long hot southern summer. Tilly was no exception as she crossed the campus with bell bottom jeans dragging the ground and her flip flops flopping. Her peasant shirt was flowing in the breeze as she crossed the street to grab a cigarette with her friends. This would not be the kids' last smoke of the day, they would gather in the bathrooms for their nicotine habit. Occasionally a teacher would shoo them out.

"Hey Tilly, heard your old lady is shacking up with Carl Davis," Jan said as she smoked her cigarette. Jan looked at Tilly through the bathroom mirror as she fixed her bangs.

"What of it." Tilly sat on the sink in the bathroom that was dark and depressing, with smoke filling it rapidly.

"Nothing, except everyone knows what a loser he is," Jan said, but cut off the conversation because of a teacher alert. The other girls scrambled to put out the cigarettes and ran into each other as they tried to get out. Tilly and Jan slowly gathered their stuff as Mrs. Wright walked in. "Tilly and Jan, go to class now," and she pointed to the door.

"Teachers are so stupid," Jan remarked thinking she was out of ear-shot of Mrs. Wright.

"They are not stupid, they just don't care," Tilly replied.

Mrs. Wright walked out of the bathroom having heard the girls' conversation. She sighed. She wanted to help her students, but it was growing more difficult to turn the tide of disrespect and discouragement. If they only knew how many sleepless nights teachers spent worrying about their students, they might appreciate the effort put in each day. Instead it was like walking into a war zone everyday. Some teachers were more dedicated than others, but all and all they tried. Mrs. Wright's thoughts went back to Tilly. She would like to get through to that one. She was bright and could go places, rise above her situation, but she needed direction. She would talk to Tilly's counselor, maybe she could help.

Carl stuck around for a lot longer than Tilly expected. She did not make life pleasant for him. There was fighting all the time, and sometimes Carl got physical. Bobby and Sis got spanked a lot and it did not matter what offense it was. Tilly thought he was too hard on them and butted heads often with him. Tilly was glad to be at work when she wasn't in school. She found it hard to study, but then homework was always optional for Tilly. Tilly was smart and could do a lot better in school if she just tried. The teachers knew this and felt they had done their best with this one. Tilly did enough to get by and that was all. Mrs. Wright had taken Tilly under her wing lately and tried to talk to her about what her options were for the future.

Home life for Tilly's family was in an uproar most of the time. Sometimes it was Bobby and Sis in trouble when it wasn't Tilly. The trouble came from too much alcohol consumed by two selfish adults.

One evening when Tilly could not borrow her mom's car, she walked to work and back home. She had asked her mom to pick her up, but that did not happen. It was a cool fall night and she enjoyed the solitary walk. She thought of Christmas, her favorite time of the year even though it was weeks away. Thanksgiving was nice, but she ended up at friends' houses a lot of times. She longed for the family gathering that unfolded in front of her each year at someone else's house. She rounded the corner to her house and heard the commotion even at that distance. The sounds were coming from her house and she rolled her eyes and mumbled to herself, "Oh no, not again." She hurried on and heard the cries of Bobby. She jumped over the loose step and went through the screen door. The main door was open because it was a warm evening even if it was early in the fall. Tilly was suddenly in the midst of a war zone. The scene before her was unfolding as if in slow motion. In the dim-lit kitchen where the light was still swinging from a blow it had received, shadows were moving as a slapping sound mixed with screams filled the house. Tilly moved on impulse to rescue her brother from the ogre that had him in his grips.

"I told you to stay out of my car, ya little brat. Ya went and put a dent in it and I'll put a dent in you!" Carl was yelling as he swung his belt trying to hit the moving target. He was clearly drunk, and wasn't hitting his mark too often, but when he did get a hit it was a success. Bobby was getting a pretty rough go of it. Tilly was in between Carl and the belt before she knew it, and received the hardest blow across her face. She swung around to see her mom wringing her hands and Sis screaming, but another painful blow caused her to faint. Bobby took the opportunity to run and Sis jumped on top of

Tilly to stop the assault. Bonnie grabbed the belt at a high risk and for the time Carl stopped and stalked out of the house.

Tilly woke up later to the smell of roses and something good cooking. She did not know where she was at first. Her vision finally focused on the vase of roses on the coffee table. She heard singing and smiled to herself - Miss June to the rescue. The hymn she was singing was familiar to Tilly and she sat up slowly.

"Oh you're awake. You took quite a lick. It was good you fainted. I had Dr. Smith come, but you don't remember. You must have been worn out to begin with for you to have slept so hard. Dr. Smith said to let you rest. Oh don't worry I called Billy and he understands more than you think," Miss June said as she went back to check the oven. Tilly did remember things last night, but it was cloudy. It was true, she had been exhausted when she had gotten home and she had found only enough strength to fight.

"Dr. Smith said you probably need some iron. I'm fixing some liver and some good vegetables. Sis is in the back room and Bobby is at home. Oh I see that look on your face. Don't worry, Carl left before the police arrived. I called them when I heard all the ruckus," Miss June said as she observed the extreme emotions going across the girl's pale face. She wanted to hug her, but Tilly was funny about that sometimes. "Why don't you go wash your face and I'll put some food on a plate for you." Tilly obeyed and made her way to the bathroom. She splashed her face with some water, and as it dripped down her arms she stopped in mid-air. She couldn't believe that she was looking at her face in the mirror. It was swollen and had a slash across the right side. Tilly carried a slight scar across her face for the rest of her life, along with scars not seen after that night.

When Tilly and Sis returned home, things were different. Some furniture was missing and the pair stopped in their tracks looking around. Bonnie walked into the room from the hall.

"Oh you're home, good," Bonnie said as she continued to walk toward the kitchen.

"Mom where is everything?" asked Sis. Tilly rolled her eyes and motioned for Sis to go to her room. Sis was looking questioningly, but left the room.

"Mom, why did he have to take things that did not belong to him?" Tilly walked into the kitchen behind her mom.

"Oh, I don't know. He was angry and just was throwing things in the truck. You know...I was afraid of him sometimes," Bonnie was saying as she was looking for something in the refrigerator. "Now, not one of your sermons...please," she said as she shut the door, unsuccessful in finding what she needed.

"He was a jerk," Tilly said as she spotted an apple on the table and grabbed it. Bonnie was looking at Tilly as she took a bite of apple.

"Let's just put this behind us, all right?" Bonnie said as she turned around to the window. Tilly could tell she was crying. Tilly walked over and put her hand on her mother's shoulder and said, "You go rest, I'll fix something to eat." Tilly was once again in the role she was comfortable in. Life continued this way for a while longer in this household.

Bonnie without a man in her life was sometimes worse than Bonnie with a man in her life. Tilly and her mom argued continually. Tilly stayed away as much as possible, and dated some. Tilly's friends did drugs and Tilly wasn't above trying things on occasion. She did want to finish school, so she would get by with what she could and still pass. She also knew she had better be straight around Billy. She often slept in class; but she managed to keep it together.

Tilly bought an old VW Beetle. It was cheap and on its last leg, but it meant more freedom. One evening Tilly had a rare night off, and she was ready to go out and kick up her heels. Her mom stopped her as she was headed out the door.

"Just where do you think you are going?" Bonnie asked as she looked Tilly over. She had her usual cigarette in one hand and a can of beer in the other. Tilly did not feel she had to answer her so she walked on.

"Hey, I asked you a question, show some respect," Bonnie said as she brushed her hair out of her eyes with the back of the hand that was holding the beer.

"I'm going out. What is it to you? You don't need a babysitter anymore." With that said, Tilly went out on the porch and the screen door slammed behind her. Bonnie opened the screen door angrily.

"Ya know, I get tired of you treatin' me like you was better than me!" Bonnie was screaming out.

"Mom, what do you want from me? I cook and clean, and I want a night away. Why do you have to start a fight?" Tilly leaped over the middle step, landed on the ground and turned around.

"Ther ya see, that's wha I mean, ya lecturing me like I was a chil." Bonnie's speech got more slurred as she drank and she was getting too worked up. Tilly ran to the fig tree and left her mom still screaming at her. She sat under the fig tree to think. It was scenes like these that made her want to leave home, but she felt she still needed to oversee the others.

It was one evening when Tilly returned home that she realized her weeks of peace were over. Carl was standing at the door. She jumped the middle loose step as usual, but she was not as perky jumping on the porch. She stopped in front of Carl wearily.

"What is it Carl?" Tilly asked.

"It's your mom. She's been calling me a lot. She is in a bad way. Well I finally had to come. I think I'll stay til she settles. She resting right now," Carl said and sipped his beer. Tilly rolled her eyes. "Carl, mom does not need you to help her settle. The authorities told you to stay away, that was the deal."

"Now Tilly, don't start up. I came because she asked me to."

"Carl, do me a favor, stay away from me." With that Tilly shoved past him. When she came into the house, she saw his suitcase.

"Well I see you've made yourself at home," Tilly said and walked on to her room. Sis stuck her head out of her door. The look on her face said it all, and Tilly gave her a hug. They said good-night and left it at that. Tilly went to sleep so fast, she did not have time to think about the situation.

Carl being back put a strain on the already volatile household. Tilly had a mouth on her and it got her in a lot of trouble. She came between Bobby and Carl often. She was getting tired of it; and getting in trouble at school.

Tilly and Carl had words again one day. It was when a teacher called concerned about Tilly. She had skipped a few classes and missed a test. Bonnie, in a rare moment of clarity, became upset. Carl tried to calm her down and then turned on Tilly. The usual "You are not my father," came out of Tilly's mouth before she ran to her room and picked a few things to put in her oversized bag. She did not know where she was going, but she wanted out for a while and she would teach them all a lesson or two. She walked out and hopped off the porch and went to her car. She tried to crank it, but it did not crank. Tilly got out of the car and slammed the door. She looked back at the house. She could see her mom through the window wringing her hands and crying. Carl was yelling. She decided she couldn't go back in the house. She grabbed her bag and headed down the road. She heard Carl saying, "Well she won't go far, the car didn't start." She heard her mom yelling at

Carl, "Go get her Carl. It sounds like a storm a'comin."

"Oh Bon, stop it woman, go get me a beer. I said she will be back." He plopped on the sofa heavily. Bonnie, still wringing her hands, obeyed Carl and went in the kitchen. She glanced out of the window nervously.

Tilly was walking past Miss June's wondering if she should go in, but decided not to disturb her. She continued on. She heard a car behind her.

"Hey pretty girl!" Tilly rolled her eyes. She knew who the voice belonged to before she turned around. It was Joe Foster in his red mustang. She did not dislike Joe, but he wasn't her favorite person. He seemed to always be around.

"Hey Joe," Tilly said in a way not to give Joe a hope of any kindness.

"You want a ride - or something?" Joe said almost panting as he fixed his glasses.

"No, I'm fine. Thanks," Tilly said as she continued to walk.

"Well uh...where ya going?" he asked as a truck horn drowned out his words.

"Hey Tilly, get in. We are going over the county line to that new bar." It was Lance Hall, the most popular boy at school. He had flirted with Tilly some at school, but Tilly did not take it seriously. He was way out of her grasp. Here he was with Gary Roberts, another gorgeous human being. This was too hard for Tilly to resist and when Gary opened the door, she jumped in. Joe watched her jump in the truck with the other boys. He pushed his glasses up and drove on. Tilly was in between the guys wondering why she had just gotten in the truck. She was thinking that it wasn't a good idea, but said nothing.

"Since this county is so backward and still dry, ya know... well we just thought we would check out the bar over the line. Hey, well, why not? Let's party!" It was Lance talking, leering at Tilly. Gary was looking her over pretty well too. This was not the attention she was looking for. The boys were already high on something, and Tilly wanted to get out, but it was raining too hard and there was no shelter on this country road. She did not want to be put out in the middle of nowhere, but she wasn't sure she was any safer in the truck.

"Wow look at that!" It was Gary, talking and pointing ahead. Tilly looked up to see a funnel cloud.

"A tornado!" Lance yelled. "We need to find a ditch!"

"No, let's keep going!" yelled Gary, clearly fascinated with the whole event.

"Are you crazy? Pull over Lance, There's a ditch!" Tilly screamed, wide-eyed, thinking she was seeing her last moments on earth. Gary got out a camera in Lance's glove compartment. They tried to get out of the truck at once, and Gary was trying to take a picture. "Would you move it!" Tilly yelled pushing Gary. That was the last thing she remembered before everything went black.

She awoke confused. Tilly looked around, everything was devastated. Lance was walking around dazed. She did not see Gary right away. Something was dripping off her head and she reached up to touch it. She brought her hand down slowly and realized it was blood. She got up and stumbled around.

"Lance, where is Gary?" Tilly asked. He did not respond and she shook him.

"Uh...I uh..." and he just looked at her. She left him and looked around. She saw a pile of debris moving. Gary was flinging off the stuff and moaning. Tilly ran over to help him. She was relieved because they all looked fine. Tilly knew they all needed medical attention and she looked around for help. There were no cars in sight and no houses around. She did not know exactly where she was and she was hurt.

They all started walking without saying anything. No one led the procession, they walked in unison. They finally reached a small gas station, but the phones were out. A police car came slowly down the road and pulled into the store's parking lot. He quickly realized what had happened to the young people and called for help. The ambulance arrived and took them to the hospital.

"You were lucky," the nurse said as she applied the bandages to Tilly's head. "It took us by surprise - a lot of people were injured and there were some deaths." Tilly looked up stunned, she had not thought about her family. She leapt off the table.

"Now...now you get back up there, I have to finish this," the nurse said helping Tilly back on the table. She was a big lady with strong arms holding Tilly still.

"I have to go make a phone call," Tilly said.

"Oh, they have already made phone calls to your folks. They got all of your information," the nurse said and continued bandaging Tilly. Tilly rolled her eyes and groaned.

"What's the matter, are you in trouble?" the nurse asked. "Don't worry, they are going to be glad you are fine." There was a noise and they both looked at the door. Carl was standing in the hall looking in the room. Tilly had survived the storm outside, but she wasn't sure of the storm brewing now with Carl and Bonnie. Bonnie was making the usual motions of a caring mom in front of others, but Tilly knew this would change. Carl remained silent until they got in the car.

"Well are you satisfied?" Carl said as he slammed the car door while Tilly climbed in the backseat. Tilly stared out the window. Bonnie flipped the sun visor down and looked at herself in the mirror. "Oh, I look awful, I did not get any sleep last night." Tilly and her mom caught a glimpse of each other through the mirror and there was a hard stare down.

"I see that face, so don't get an attitude. You should be grateful you are alive. Goodness gracious, just to think what could of happened. Oh it's just upsetting." Bonnie was going on and on.

Tilly continued to look out the window.

"Some things have to change around the house...." Carl was starting up and Tilly put her head back and under her breath was saying, "blah...blah...blah..."

"What's that ya saying...uh? You had better watch it now." Carl was getting agitated and Bonnie started chatting about something else.

"Oh, I almost forgot...Billy called. I told him about the accident and he said you are not to worry, you come back to work when you're ready." Bonnie was chewing her gum and talking fast. Tilly had forgotten about work in all that had happened within the last few hours. She knew Bonnie would not forget; it was important for Tilly to bring in money to help the household.

Tilly fully recovered from her ordeal. The experience would stay with her forever. (She would learn years later that Gary Roberts never forgot about that night of the tornado either. She turned on the T.V. and there he was - a meteorologist.)

Tilly went to work the following weekend. She had missed school because of soreness and a consistent headache. She wanted to go to work and it was time. When she walked in Diane came around the counter.

"Hey girl, I was coming over today. I heard all that happened; the whole town knows. You are pretty famous. Well ya got your fifteen minutes of fame." Diane gave her a hug and noticed that Tilly winced. "Oh, you are still sore and I still see bruising." Tilly put her hand to her face. She had not thought to cover her bruises with her make-up. Diane was asking if she was all right and Tilly came out of her daze.

"Yeah, I'm fine, really." Tilly grabbed the washcloth and started to clean the tables. Billy came around the corner. "Tilly, you're okay!" He gave her a big bear hug and Tilly did not let it be known that it hurt. She knew

Billy would always be around for her and she got even busier, she did not want to cry.

Tilly was back at school the next Monday, and the rumors had flown through the school. It had not been good for Tilly's reputation to be out with the boys across county line. Girls were looking at her sideways, and the boys were leering at her.

"Hey, girl!" It was Cindy Crow behind her at her locker. Tilly turned around toward Cindy after giving her locker a hit with her fist. "Don't pay attention to them. They will soon forget...besides you were off with Gary and Lance, all the girls are jealous."

"I don't care what they think...I don't like this attention." The locker finally came open and Tilly got out what she needed. "I don't know what Gary and Lance said, but nothing happened...except of course the tornado," Tilly said and slammed the locker.

"Oh, I don't think they said anything bad about you. I think people just want to believe something bad. Barb thinks you could not possibly date either boy," Cindy said.

Tilly thought about that for a moment. Barb was the head cheerleader and had dated both boys. She was smart and beautiful. She also thought she had every boy panting after her. Maybe she did. This remark made Tilly mad. Tilly of course believed that neither of the boys would go out with her, but did not like it voiced. Barb would end up with the life she had lived, upper middle-class, college, the guy of her dreams and a successful living. Tilly wanted better too, but had blown her grades due to lack of concern, and she knew the money would not be there for college. She could hope, maybe, for community college.

Tilly had not really lived up to the reputation that had been bestowed on her by her fellow classmates, but was rapidly headed in that direction on her own self-destructive path. As her own self-worth went downward, so did she. She wanted love and looked for it in the wrong places and with the wrong people.

Graduation was coming fast. It was Tilly's last school year. She had not fared well with her grades and had given up on college. Billy had talked about teaching her all the ropes at work so she could manage, but she was changing. Tilly had lost her favorite cousin Jake to a car accident. This had a lot to do with her changing attitude. She was living carelessly, dating anyone, and doing anything. Her mother and Carl just added to her daily torture.

Carl often borrowed her car after losing his own recently to debt. That left Tilly to catch a ride or walk to work and school. One such day, Sonny Willis drove up beside her as she was walking home from work.

"Hey, girl!" Sonny stopped next to her in his green Camaro.

"Wow, nice car!" Tilly said. She had not seen Sonny in a year. He had dropped out of school and was working as a mechanic, making good money. He was a few years older than Tilly and he was wild. Tilly did not care, she liked him. She was almost home and Sonny pulled into her driveway ahead of her. She looked up and her eyes caught the sight of her little VW Bug. It was squashed. Her mouth flew open.

"Wow, what happened? Is this why you're walking?" Sonny asked as he kicked the back tire and spit out some tobacco. Tilly looked at Sonny and her car with disgust. Her life was depressing. Carl came out of the house waving his arms.

"Now Tilly, that piece of junk caused me to wreck today. I could've been killed. Stupid little car, it's totaled. Too bad we don't have insurance to replace it, but that is life."

Tilly looked at Carl and the old saying came to his mind, "If looks could kill..."

"Ya just ruined my life!" Tilly yelled.

"Now Tilly, don't get worked up," Carl said throwing his hand up in the air.

"Sonny wait, I'm coming with you! I'll be right back," Tilly yelled as she ran in the house. When she came out of the house, she had on a very short skirt and a skimpy top. These were clothes she had kept hidden at Diane's apartment over Billy's place.

"Wait just a minute! What is that you have on?" It was Bonnie, who had just pulled up to the curb and was getting out of her car. She was questioning her daughter's choice of attire.

"I'm leaving with Sonny and we are going to have fun. I don't know when I'll be back," Tilly said defiantly.

"Now Tilly, I know you're mad with the car and all..." Bonnie was trying to smooth things over, but Tilly got into the car and slammed the door. Sonny was speechless as he started backing out of the driveway. Sis ran up to the car window where Tilly sat. Sis was fourteen and emotional. Her pretty face showed the fear she felt as she grabbed the car.

"You are coming back, aren't you?" Sis was panting.

"I always do," and she turned to Sonny and nodded to go. Sonny sped out leaving the people in the yard with their mouths open. Where they were going no one knew. Tilly just wanted to get away.

"Carl is a creep," Tilly said when they had driven in silence for a while.

"Well I've known Carl for a long time. He is trouble. He lives off people as long as they let him," Sonny said.

"So, I hear you're trouble too." Tilly looked slyly at him.

"Oh yeah, what else do they say?" Sonny had a smirk on his face.

"Well let's see...that you are a hard worker, but should have stayed in school. They say you have the business running pretty good and..." Tilly rolled her eyes.

"And... what?" Sonny was now curious. He grabbed Tilly's knee when she wouldn't answer and she screamed with laughter.

"That you are a bit wild," Tilly screamed out laughing.

"What do you think?" Sonny asked seriously.

"I don't know. I guess I will find out," Tilly said playing with her necklace.

"Where do you want to go?" Sonny asked realizing that they were aimlessly driving around.

"I don't know, maybe back to Miss June's house or Diane's." Tilly was contemplating more than giving an answer.

"Miss June, wow I have not thought about her in years. She used to be my first grade

teacher. She still live next door to you?"
Sonny asked.

"Yes, she has been a second mother to me. I
can talk to her about anything. She knows
everything about me," Tilly said. Sonny
nodded and continued to drive.

"Let's eat," Sonny declared. He pulled into
the burger place. Tilly felt like she could eat
too, so she agreed. They went into the small
dinning area after they got the order and once
again sat in silence and ate.

"So where do you want to go?" Sonny asked
again, but he wasn't anxious to let Tilly go.

"Take me to Diane's. I'll stay there til
morning," Tilly said reaching for a greasy fry.

"Don't go, stay with me. I have the
apartment over my body shop." Sonny took a
big bite of the hamburger he had been
devouring and shrugged.

"Oh, I had better not," Tilly said shyly. She
knew that would cause talk, not that she
cared much. Sonny was older and not bad-
looking. He had a muscular build with light
brown hair and deep blue eyes. She did look
at him differently that evening. He became
her "Knight in Shinning Armor."

Tilly decided to go to Diane's, but was with
Sonny most of the two days she stayed away
from home. Her mother knew where she was,
due to Billy's kind concern about the

situation. He did not think that Bonnie should suffer not knowing where her daughter was. He felt sorry for Bonnie, but at the same time felt she should be a better mother to her children.

Tilly went back home to prepare for graduation. Bonnie was subdued and Carl avoided her altogether. She planned on moving out for good after graduation. She had also decided to date Sonny despite everyone's objections. To her Sonny was a good guy and was good to her.

"Sonny is a bit wild," Diane said when Tilly hit the door at work after being dropped off by Sonny.

"Oh and hello to you too," Tilly said as she swiped her purse toward Diane playfully. Tilly turned around and declared, "I'm in love." Diane's jaw flew open and Billy came around the counter.

"Now Tilly, don't go gettin involved with that boy or man as he truly is. Tilly you'll be hurt mighty awful. He can't stay with one woman and he is a good deal older than you." Billy was beside himself, surely his little Tilly won't fall for the wildest boy the town had.

"He is only six years older than me," Tilly said. She couldn't believe her happy day was being destroyed.

"Yeah, but you are only seventeen," Billy said.

"I'm almost eighteen," Tilly shouted back and left the two standing where they were. Billy and Diane exchanged looks.

When Tilly got to the back room to put her things away, her confidence left her. She sat in the chair and felt drained. She put her face in her hands and cried. Sonny made her feel special and that is all she wanted. No one understood.

"Hey Tilly!" It was Jan coming up from behind her at the locker at school.

"Hey." Tilly was trying to unlock her bottom locker and it was sticking again.

"Where ya staying? Callie said you moved out. Oh!" Jan exclaimed, and Tilly jumped up to find out what was the matter. "I broke my nail...ah...I wanted them to look good for graduation." Jan was examining her broken nail as Tilly turned around and kicked her locker shut.

"What's the matter?" Jan asked with her finger in her mouth.

"Everyone is in my business," Tilly replied and walked away.

"Hey, it is almost graduation and you should be happy!" Jan said, excited as she was scurrying after Tilly.

"Well I'm not. Everyone is going away to college. What do I have to look forward to? Even you are going," Tilly said and kept walking.

"Just to Jr. College...we can't afford anything else. I wish I could leave like Callie Cole," She said making motions as if she were fixing her hair and turning side to side.

"Look at me, I'm Miss Beauty Queen and I'm just better than anyone else. I get to go away to the University of Georgia...cause my ole man went there..." Jan was talking in the most southern drawl she could conjure up, and she was prancing around. When she was turning around she missed her step and fell right in front of her victim. Callie looked down at her.

"Jan what in the world..." Everyone was laughing. Callie was trying to figure out what was going on, and somehow got the idea they were laughing at her rather then Jan. She had missed the earlier dialog, but the others in the hall had heard most of it. Callie looked at Tilly questioningly. Tilly just shook her head and walked on. Jan trotted up behind her again, and Tilly thought she would never shake her. She liked Jan, but today she wanted peace and quiet.

"That was close," Jan said when she caught up with Tilly.

"You know you shouldn't do that," Tilly said.

"Do what?" Jan asked innocently.

"Your impressions of people...you are good, but they could hurt someone's feelings," Tilly scolded. When she reached her classroom Tilly stopped Jan from going on.

"Jan...I have not moved out. I might move in with Diane after graduation. I was only gone a couple of days," Tilly said.

"Oh, well I guess the other part is rumor too." Jan shrugged and started to walk away.

"What other part?" Tilly grabbed her arm and the bell rang.

"That you are dating Sonny, the gas station man hunk,"

"It's not a gas station, it is a body shop."

"It is true!" And Jan ran off. Tilly turned in the doorway to an audience. The class was poking each other and giggling at the girls' conversation. Mrs. May didn't think it was funny. Tilly slid into her desk with Mrs. May eyeing her. She would be lucky not to get a day after school for this.

Chapter 6

Spring 1978

It was graduation day. Tilly was gathering up her things. She had decided to meet Jan at her house. She knew Carl and her mom were not planning to attend her graduation ceremony. Bobby and Sis wanted to come, but she couldn't get them there herself. Sis and Bobby at fifteen and thirteen still depended a great deal on Tilly. She worried about them. What would they do without her if she moved out? Tilly knew that they were the reason she had stuck things out. She was roused out of her thoughts when she glanced at the clock. She quickly swept up her things and ran out of the house. Tilly leaped over the middle step and continued. She had to walk to Jan's house, but it wasn't far. The summer was well upon them even in the first week of June. She smelled the honeysuckles that reminded her every year at this time that school would soon be out. She passed the fig tree and touched a leaf. A bee buzzed past and she stopped to pick up a fallen magnolia flower. She always did that when she walked past that magnolia tree at the edge of Miss June's yard. She then wondered if Miss June had made it back in town. Her brother was sick and she had to go to see him. She had been afraid it might be serious. Tilly had not heard from her and hoped that all was well. The magnolia's lemon-like smell sent her on her way as she took a big sniff of the white blossom in her hand. She touched the petals and dreamed about the future. Sonny had spoken of coming, but she wasn't holding her breath on that one. He was distant lately and she wondered if what people said about him was true. Her heart still felt a pang when she thought of him. A car horn blew and she looked over to see Jan in her beat up old VW Beetle. Tilly ran over to the window.

"I thought I was meeting you at your house," Tilly yelled.

"I wanted to be sure we got there early enough. Get in!" Jan waved Tilly into the car. Tilly got in and they took off with the music blasting. Jan was a fun person to be around. She made Tilly laugh, and she needed that. She had known Jan all her life, but only recently became best friends with her. Tilly had a hard time having close friendships and her circle of friends was always small. Tilly always hated a giggly bunch of girls. She was a deep thinker. She was bored at normal girly things and therefore kept to herself or found a like-minded individual. Jan fit that description. Jan was from a broken home and was left alone a lot. This gave plenty of unsupervised time to get into all sorts of things in the past year. They had skipped school some and smoked marijuana together. The good part of it was that both girls had to work and go to school, so the time to play was brief. Perhaps that saved them from future grief. The two in the car going down the street with the music loud this day looked like a couple of normal teenagers, but they had a future to consider and decisions to make in their lives.

The little rusted gray beetle bug on wheels came to a stop at the stop sign. It made a sputtering sound and gave out. The music was still blaring out, but the groans from the girls inside could be heard.

"Will this thing get us there?" Tilly asked. It was hot inside the still car and Tilly was losing her patience as Jan frantically tried to bring life back to the bug.

"Oh it's getting late. Go ahead and put your robe and hat on so we can run in," Jan said while still turning the key with no results. "Get out and push a little!"

Tilly was adjusting her hat and the gold tassel was swinging.

"What! No way!" Tilly shot back. Jan gave her a hard look and Tilly got out of the car. She was now fully attired for graduation and she was pushing a stupid little car. She was hoping no one would see this, but was hoping for help as well. She pushed the car and nothing happened.

"It's dead," Jan said bluntly when Tilly came around to the window. Tilly sighed and leaned on the back of the car. Jan got out of the car.

"You know, this tops my life," Tilly said.

"Well don't take it personal. Let's push it out of the way. There is a parking lot." Jan pointed to the small day-care parking lot to their right.

"You're kidding!" Tilly rolled her eyes at Jan. "Great, I can't even manage to make it to my own graduation." Tilly pushed the little car while Jan had the driver's side door open with her left leg out trying to work the wheel and push with her one foot. Tilly's forgotten tasseled hat slid down her forehead when she laughed.

"What are you laughing at?" Jan yelled back.

"You look like Fred Flintstone trying to get to work...you know... the cartoon,"

Tilly was out of breath as they were turning it into the parking space.

"Well who are you? Barney?" Jan said as she got out of the car.

"I would prefer to be Wilma," Tilly kidded back.

"Yeah she and Betty have a body...uh," Jan was laughing at her joke.

"We can't make it on time walking, but we are going to have to start. Maybe we can catch a ride," Tilly said optimistically.

"Well, I took the back way and it is longer. Chances are slim we will see anyone," Jan said. Tilly wanted to fuss, but refrained since she knew that Jan felt better in the neighborhood back roads with her unreliable car. Getting on the busy streets could have been dangerous. Both girls started down the sidewalk.

"Anyone coming to see you graduate?" Tilly asked after a while of silence.

"Just Mom and my sister. Dad is ... well gone. I haven't seen him for a while. Who is coming for you?" Jan asked.

"No one," Tilly said softly.

"Sonny's not coming?" Jan asked and Tilly laughed.

"I think Sonny's allergic to school," Tilly said as she fiddled with the tassel of her hat.

"Yeah, I would say so...since he didn't stay long enough to graduate," Jan said leaning against Tilly. Jan reached in her purse for some gum and held out a piece for Tilly.

"No thanks, I could use a cigarette," Tilly said and looked through her purse.

"Do you have one?" Tilly asked after an unsuccessful search.

"No, I was afraid to bring them. I do want to graduate...you know," Jan scolded and looked back hoping for a car to come. Tilly was singing a favorite song of theirs and Jan listened.

"You know, Tilly, you have a great voice," Jan said, but Tilly just smiled and kept on singing. Tilly had gotten into chorus at school, but had to quit in order to work after school. Tilly was disappointed when they had moved the practice session from before school to after school. She now only sang in her room or in her car.

"Ya know, that new movie with your favorite actor is out," Jan said after a few minutes of silence.

"How do you know who my favorite actor is?" Tilly asked, put out with Jan.

"I can see. Besides I was there when you bought that huge poster. Where did you put that poster anyway?" Jan asked, stopping to adjust her shoe. "Aw...my feet are hurting, where are the cars?" There was more silence. After a while Tilly broke the silence.

"It's packed away with my stuff to go to Diane's."

"What's packed away?" Jan stumbled and held on to Tilly. Tilly rolled her eyes. Jan had the attention span of a goldfish.

"Besides I like Tim Reynolds for his acting ability," Tilly said.

"Yeah right, Tim Reynolds has a lot more to admire besides his acting ability. He is an older man Tilly, think you could handle him?" Tilly started to defend herself further, but a car horn blew behind them. Tilly's face lit up when she saw who was behind the wheel of the so familiar Buick. Sis and Bobby were hanging out the car window waving and Miss June was smiling.

"Get in!" Miss June yelled. It did not take a further invitation for the girls to leap into the car. Hot and tired, Tilly fell into the front seat pushing Sis over in the middle. Jan got in the back pushing Bobby over.

"We saw the dead Bug back there," Bobby said looking at Jan.

"I was worried when Bobby spotted Jan's car and there was no sign of ya'll," Miss June said.

"What made you come this way to the school?" Tilly asked Miss June.

"I told her this is the way Jan came all the time," Sis said.

"The Lord must have guided Sis this way and I was in no hurry, but you are going to be late." Miss June looked at her watch.

"Tell me about it," Jan said.

"I'm so glad you are back. I thought you had to be with your brother. Is he better or..." Tilly did not pursue that line of thought.

"He is better now. We secured a nurse for him at home and I will be going to check on him frequently. I couldn't miss my girl's graduation unless I absolutely had to," Miss June said. The look that was exchanged between Tilly and Miss June said volumes. Tilly felt loved and cared for, and Miss June had someone to care for. Tilly looked at Sis and Bobby. Sis had a new dress and Bobby a new pair of pants. Tilly knew where the clothes had come from. Miss June kept a closet with clothes for the kids in it. She knew when they needed something on occasions like this.

They pulled into the parking lot and Miss June stopped at the door where there was a sea of green robes with legs walking around.

"Well this looks like where you should be, maybe you can blend in," Miss June said. The girls jumped out. Mrs. Lyons was looking frantically out of the glass windows. Everyone was getting in line.

"Girls, where have you been? You have missed everything that we went over. Get in line quickly and ask what to do. Tilly, get rid of that gum!" Tilly quickly did as she was told and fixed her hat. Mrs. Lyons fluttered around and fanned herself.

"I don't know how many more years I can take this." She was talking to whoever listened, but it was not lost on Tilly. She felt bad that she had helped put her in this state of anxiety.

"All right, I hear the music. Now march the way you practiced." Mrs. Lyons clapped her hands and motioned them on. They began to walk. Tilly was walking at a clip when Tommy turned around to her and told her to slow down. She complied. Tilly was thinking, This was it! The moment! She had no idea what lay ahead, just like thousands of young students across the nation and over the years every June. Tilly would reflect upon this moment many times years from now.

Chapter 7

Fall 1978

Tilly finally moved in with Diane after graduation. She no longer wanted to go back home. She felt she had abandoned Sis and Bobby, but they were getting old enough to make their own decisions. They had Miss June as an anchor, and that would have to be enough for now. Tilly was carefree for the first time in her life.

Carl was in and out of Bonnie's life. He never bought Tilly another car. Tilly worked and saved to buy an old brown Comet with a vinyl top. It was ugly, but functional. She didn't find herself needing a car quite so much living above the diner and dating Sonny all the time.

Tilly's new lifestyle lent itself to a world of trouble; and it came. She was going too fast with Sonny and she found herself in more trouble. She was to make a decision that would alter her life forever.

"Get an abortion," Sonny said as they were together one evening after Tilly told him her news. "I'll pay for it and take you."

"No, I don't want to get an abortion. I have a friend who got one and she regrets it." Tilly

got up and paced around sobbing. The small apartment was even smaller right now and the room was closing in on her. She wiped her tears.

"Why can't we just get married?" Tilly asked desperately. Sonny rolled his eyes and Tilly jerked around to face him.

"You are a jerk!" she yelled. Sonny held up his hands and shook his head.

"We already talked about this," and he walked away. Sonny loved his life and he did not want to get married, that was clear. The door slammed and she heard his footfalls going down the steps. The apartment was silent. Tilly was alone with her fears and torment.

Tilly put off dealing with her "problem." She had no intention of doing as Sonny asked, but decided to go to the clinic for advice. She couldn't bring herself to talk to Miss June. Shame hugged her closely and that was hard. Her mother would only yell as any hypocrite would. Her imagination played out all the scenes that could take place with mention of this to anyone in her life. She couldn't care less what her mom thought, but Billy and Miss June were another matter. Billy was so good to her, she hated to disappoint him. Her head was spinning and her emotions high. What would she do? When Tilly threw up a few times and looked pale, Diane knew what was up. She advised Tilly to go to the clinic. Diane had had an abortion once.

Tilly walked into the cold clinic. The door creaked and slammed behind her and she jumped. The waiting room was full, and she lost herself taking in the scene before her. There were women and young girls everywhere and they all seemed to be looking at her. She clutched her purse with both hands and walked toward the desk.

"May I help you?" The woman behind the desk was repeating the question before Tilly was roused out of her daze. The red-headed attractive woman smiled at her. Tilly moved closer to her as if to let her in on a secret. She leaned over the desk.

"I want to speak to someone about..." Tilly hesitated and looked around. She cleared her voice and turned back around to the woman. She could not get the words out.

"Sign right here." The lady pushed the clip board in front of her and nodded as if in understanding. Tilly took the clip board and signed her name. She felt faint.

"Maybe you had better sit down, you look pale." The red-head got up and reached out to her. "Are you all right? Are you in any pain or discomfort now?" The lady looked concerned.

"No, I'm okay. Thanks, I'll just sit down," Tilly replied and found a seat.

Tilly walked out of the clinic a while later. She had borrowed Sonny's car. He was working at the body shop. She had to take the car back to him. Tilly got into the car and put her head down. The words of the doctor came ringing back to her in her head over and over again.

"Sorry, you have waited too long to come here. If you want to look into adoption, there are people here who can give you information. We have counselors available through the state that you can talk to and get some advice and direction." Doctor Libb kept talking, and Tilly looked up only to notice he had his hand on the doorknob as if to make a quick exit. He couldn't care less and Tilly knew it at that moment. He was off to another patient in his mind and he had many to see. Tilly wanted to leave this place as quickly as possible. The doctor opened the door and turned around. "You don't need anything else do you?" The body language spoke volumes and Tilly looked him in the eyes and clearly said, "No." When the door shut and the nurse was left cleaning things, Tilly's eyes filled with tears. The nurse did not even notice.

"You can get dressed now," the nurse instructed, and without looking at Tilly, went out the door. The scene had played again in her mind as she sat in the car. She started the car, feeling confused and sad. She was glad that one decision was left out of her hands, but she was scared of Sonny. He had wanted her to "take care" of everything. He had given her enough money and sent her on her way. She hated him right now.

When she arrived at the body shop, she pulled into the pot-holed parking lot. The smell of grease, oil and gas permeated the air. She sank back into the seat, sick to her stomach. Sonny was working on a car when he looked up and saw her. Tilly got slowly out of the car and went over to the grass. She fell to her knees and threw-up.

"What happened?" Sonny was bending over her. "Did they do it? You were supposed to call. I would have jumped into the truck and helped you home." Tilly turned to him and pushed him away.

"They said it was too late," Tilly said as she grabbed her purse and pulled out a tissue. She wiped her face. Sonny felt sorry for her at that moment and hugged her.

"Well that puts a whole new spin on things," he said as he held her, and Tilly let him hold her. She wanted to hit him over and over again, but she was silent. When they got upstairs in the small apartment, Tilly broke the silence.

"They gave me some information on adoption," she said bluntly. Sonny turned around from the sink.

"No...no, I won't have a stranger raise a child of mine!" Sonny's exclamation startled Tilly. She walked over to Sonny and he nodded. No words were needed. They hugged.

Chapter 8

1978-1979

Tilly and Sonny were wed on a weekend without much fanfare. They went to the court house and it was done. Diane came and one of Sonny's friends, but that was it. No one approved of this match. Even Tilly knew she would not have married Sonny had things been different, but that was that. Tilly moved into the small garage apartment of Sonny's above the shop. She went to work everyday and got bigger. Billy fussed over her

"I'm fine," Tilly declared one day when she had to sit down a moment. Billy had quickly been at her side. Diane stopped what she was doing and came over. "I just needed to sit a minute. I feel like I'm a ton. You two go on and work." She waved Billy and Diane away. She did not like a fuss. Tilly could tell they were looking at her from the corners of their eyes.

Tilly put her head down and wished she could turn back time. Sonny wasn't a pleasant person, and she did not love him. She doubted he loved her. He had been indifferent to her lately, and preoccupied. She suspected there was someone else. Sonny was always a womanizer. She came back to herself and got up to wait on the couple that had come in.

Tilly poured everything out to Miss June. Miss June did what she always did - she prayed. She tried to talk to Bobby and Sis about things too, but they were not as close to her. She worried over the kids all the time. Bobby had gotten picked up for shoplifting and Sis skipped school a lot. Even though Tilly had left home, she still had to deal with those two. She had to pay the fine for Bobby's shoplifting charge and she talked to Sis's school about her failing grades. Miss June helped as much as she could. Bonnie was too involved with her own problems to be any help.

At work Tilly was slowing down. She could still chew her gum at a rapid rate, but the rest of her was having a hard time getting around to the tables. Billy tried to alleviate some of the work-load. He hired his daughter Cindy to help. She was old enough now and was doing a good job. Billy worried about his young daughter after having seen what Diane and Tilly got into. He knew that their upbringing was the cause of most of their grief in life and their poor choices. Cindy seemed strong and he did not let it worry him too much, but he kept a tight rein on her. He kept a close eye on all his "girls."

Sonny became more and more apart from Tilly. He was out a lot and sometimes did not show up until morning. He started shoving her often, and he yelled at her all the time. Tilly was hoping for things to be different when the baby arrived. For the most part she allowed Sonny his life and she lived hers. The upstairs apartment diminished in size as time passed. The walls closed in on her and she stayed away as long as she could. She and Sonny moved around each other instead of with each other.

Tilly sometimes lost herself in the movies. She liked to read, but found it difficult to concentrate. A movie allowed her to lose herself for a while. She still adored her favorite actor, Tim Reynolds. He was at least ten years older than she was, but Tilly thought the older he got the handsomer he got. She dreamed of meeting him one day. She admired his family. He was a rarity in Hollywood with a good solid married life and two kids. Tilly would always admire this characteristic above all others in a man. She would never have that, and she would have to make the best of her life as it was.

The baby decided to come on a bleak cold morning. It was Valentine's Day and winter still wanted to hang on. It turned rainy, and as in the south when rain and freezing temperatures mix, ice forms. It hangs on the trees and power lines, but worst of all it creates a layer of unseen ice on the streets. It is called black ice. It was such a day that labor pains hit Tilly. Sonny warmed the car and helped Tilly into the front seat. He drove a while before they heard the familiar ping on the windows.

"It's sleeting," Sonny said.

"Oh, I hope we can make it. You need to hurry," Tilly said in pain.

"I'm trying," Sonny shot back.

One thing about black ice is that you can't see it, and Sonny hit some suddenly. He tried the brakes and they kept going.

"Sonny, don't brake, turn the wheels!" Tilly yelled.

"I can't!" Sonny yelled back and the car was out of control. They ended up in a ditch. Tilly was groaning and fussing at Sonny. Tilly felt wetness and she looked down.

"Oh, no!" Tilly yelled.

"What!" Sonny threw up his arms.

"I think my water broke!"

"How did that happen?"

"Sonny, you are asking me how this happened? I can't believe you. Do you know anything?" Tilly bent over clutching her belly.

"What does that mean?" Sonny asked and Tilly shot him a look that hushed him up.

"It's coming," Tilly said.

"Well how do you know? I mean...you haven't had a baby before. First babies take a long time...ya know." Sonny was scared and talking fast. Tilly reached over and hit him. Once she hit him she hit him again and again. She was taking everything out on him right then, and she lost control. He became her target. Sonny soon fled out of the car.

"Come back...ya stupid jerk! This baby is coming!"

"Tilly, stop it! You can't have that baby right now! "Sonny yelled through the window. He wasn't getting back in.

"Stop it? You think I can stop it? There is a car coming...get help!" Tilly pointed at the road.

"Just calm down, I'll get help!" Sonny was relieved to see a possible helper. He could not take this much longer. The frozen precipitation continued and they were miserable.

"The car is slowing down... and I think it's stopping. I'll try to get them to help. Stay put," Sonny said and walked toward the car. Tilly shook her head at Sonny's lack of courage right now. He slipped and fell as he was walking toward the car. A man emerged from the car. Sonny observed chains on the man's tire as he was picking himself up from the fall.

"Sir, I think my wife is having her baby...uh right now... I guess... I don't know." Sonny was stammering and cold. The man peered in the window at Tilly.

"Did your water break?" He asked.

"Yes...I think so." Tilly bent over again in pain.

"Don't worry, I'm a doctor at Watkins. You headed to Liberty or Watkins?"

"Sir, it don't matter right now, but Watkins is where we were going," Sonny replied.

"Good, lets get her into the back of my car. I've got some blankets in the trunk. Don't worry...I think we can make it," said the doctor. They were on each side of Tilly helping her to the Mercedes. Sonny slid in beside her and the doctor drove slowly down the road. It was the longest few minutes in Tilly's life.

Tilly gave birth to a baby girl thirty minutes after arriving at Watkins Hospital. Sonny stayed long enough to see Tilly in her room resting. He made some excuse about getting back to the shop. Tilly's mom called and said she did not feel like coming to the hospital in the bad weather, but that she would come by when she got home. The next day Diane came by with balloons; and Billy's wife Edna came by with flowers and a message from Billy. Cindy came with her mom. Edna was nice and was devoted to her family. It had been hard on her when they lost their son in Vietnam. She had stayed close to home and seldom left. Cindy was opening and closing the blinds at the hospital window and gazing out as if in deep thought.

"She is the only one left at home now. It is times like these that bring back memories." Edna looked sad and Tilly took her hand. "You know, I was thinking, Cindy and I could baby sit if you would like," Edna gained control of herself and smiled.

"That would be so nice." Tilly looked over at Cindy and she looked pleased.

"I like babies," Cindy said.

"Good that is settled. You let us know. We will let you rest now." Edna and Cindy left and Tilly was alone. No one was in the bed next to her. Miss June had called to say she would be by the next day. Tilly couldn't wait to show off Rae Dawn. Where she got that name she couldn't say, but it came to her and sounded good, so it stuck. Sonny didn't seem to mind what she called the baby, and stayed away until it was time to pick up Tilly from the hospital.

Tilly figured Sonny had been drunk for a couple of days. He had started drinking too much lately and she worried about that. Tilly knew part of it was the financial responsibility he now had on him. Tilly decided to go back to work as soon as possible to help alleviate the problem. Sis had started working at Billy's. She had quit school, but promised Billy to finish night school and get her G.E.D. When she enrolled in the night school program, Billy felt better about giving her a job. He wanted all his "girls" to have their education. He even had encouraged Tilly to go to the Jr. College. Diane, he had given up on. Sis now wanted to keep Rae so Tilly could work some shifts at Billy's. They were able to work out a plan. Tilly was concerned about Sis's commitment, but she had no choice. Sonny was seldom home, even with the shop below them. He often went out at night. Rae cried a lot and Tilly knew Sonny wanted to be away from the small, and now loud, apartment. She wanted to get away too at times.

Two months after Rae was born, Tilly allowed Sis to come and take care of her. It worked better than Tilly expected and this continued for a while. Sonny drank more often and the business suffered. He was becoming unreliable. Tilly did not let Sonny's bad habits bother her. She led her own life and went out with her friends who were single. She still loved the movies and her favorite actor. She smoked and drank more. Rae was growing before her very eyes and proved to be a hand-full. She was strong-willed even as young as she was.

Chapter 9

1981

Jan was there one day as Rae chattered away. She started talking early and repeated things quickly. It was a rare morning off for Tilly, and it was a pleasant time. She moved into her own apartment and she was at peace.

"So, when is the divorce final?" Jan asked.

"Soon," Tilly replied grabbing things out of the refrigerator to make sandwiches.

"Chat noo ga..chat noo ga..." Rae was chanting.

"What is she saying?" Jan finally asked.

"Chattanooga, she heard it on T.V. She loves words that sound good to say. She will latch on to words she likes and repeat them." Tilly got a cookie and handed it to Rae. Rae was on a pad in the small living room and it was open to the kitchen. She was busy playing with her favorite toys.

"Sounds like she is very smart," Jan observed.

"Yeah, I wonder where she gets it from. It is scary," Tilly laughed.

"Well she didn't get it from Stupid Head Sonny," Jan said and they both rolled in laughter.

"Stupid head... stupid head..." Rae was now chanting again.

"Shush, I think we need to watch what we say around her," Tilly said and continued to laugh without Rae seeing her. Jan finally wiped her eyes and asked.

"How is Sis working out, living here with you and working at Billy's?"

"We have it worked out. She is at work when I'm home and when she is here, I'm working. She got her G.E.D," Tilly answered.

"That is good," Jan said.

"Well this way I don't have to deal with the attitude she gets sometimes. She really doesn't like it when she has a date and Sonny doesn't show up for his weekend if I am working." Tilly walked over and got Rae and wiped her mouth.

"Anything is better than living with Carl though. I would call him something, but not with the little one repeating everything," Jan said with a laugh. Tilly nodded in agreement.

"I can keep Rae sometime, if you need help and Sis has a date." Jan took Rae and bounced her.

"Oh, I wouldn't let Sis know that, but maybe sometime," Tilly said.

"Hey, are you going to the new Tim Reynolds movie that is out?" Jan turned her head,

knowing this got to Tilly. She liked to tease
her on this subject.

"Oh...stop it!" Tilly said giving Jan a light
push.

"Stop it....Stop it..." Rae again chanted.
They both laughed again.

Chapter 10

1982

Tilly drove into her mom's driveway and hesitated getting out of the car. Her mom had asked her to come over, and she wondered what she was up to. Tilly got Rae out of her car seat and walked toward the porch. Rae ran ahead and went up the steps. When she got to the loose middle step she pounced on it as if it were a game.

"Rae, get off that step before you fall!" Tilly said grabbing up Rae. She looked up to see Bobby smoking on the front porch. He was in the newly installed porch swing. His mother had always wanted one, so he had put it up for her. He was looking rather smug.

"Those kill ya." Rae toddled up to Bobby.

"Tell ya mom that." Bobby replied.

"She does," Tilly said. "Where is mom?"

"In the house," Bobby said. Getting much more of a conversation out of Bobby would have been unusual. She never knew what Bobby was thinking.

They went through the creaky screen door. It was a hot May day and the house was a little warm. The screen door allowed some breeze in.

"Mom!" Tilly yelled out. Rae ran to the chair where there was a stack of stuffed animals. She was pulling them off the chair one by one and dropping them on the floor. Tilly saw her mom in the kitchen smoking and cooking something. Tilly rolled her eyes.

"Carl's gone again," Tilly stated after making a quick observation.

"About a week. I think there is someone else." Bonnie was stirring something on the stove and she did not turn around.

"Mom, there was always someone else," Tilly shot back. Bonnie put down her spoon, pointed her cigarette at Tilly and gave her a look. Tilly shrugged.

"You know you shouldn't let Bobby smoke. He is too young," Tilly said as she picked a cracker out of the box on the table and bit into it. Bonnie slammed a drawer and turned around.

"Tilly, how old were you when you started smoking? Who are you kidding? That is like the pot calling the kettle black." Bonnie continued puttering around looking for some unknown object. Tilly bit her lip trying to gain control.

"Smells good," Tilly said after a short silence.

"Spaghetti, ya favorite," Bonnie smiled. Now Tilly did ask herself what her mom was up to.

Too nice, meant something she wanted from Tilly.

Tilly was driving home reflecting on the visit. Rae slipped into a nap and the music on the radio was playing softly. Her mom had set a trap for her and she fell into it.

Bonnie had needed money. Tilly shook her head. She had given her some and was thankful she had it to give. "Oh well," she said to herself as she turned up the music and kept beat with it on the steering wheel. She wasn't going to let it worry her. Tilly had a rare date the next night and she would make plans for that. She had met him when she waited on his table. Brian was nice, not too bright, but safe. Yeah, she would go out and kick up her heels. But it wasn't long before Tilly once again had to deal with her Mom.

"Bobby moved out." The voice on the other end of the phone was helpless and frail.

"Mom, what did you expect? He quit school and found friends just like him. I guess he moved into that old house at the edge of town with those guys...uh." Tilly replied not surprised at any of this. She was fixing three-year-old Rae a sandwich.

"Tilly, since Sis took off with that man to Florida, it must be hard making ends meet. I know things have to be tight...ya know...to pay a babysitter and all," Bonnie was saying.

"What are you getting at Mom?" Tilly shot back.

"Well you could move here...rent free...ya know. I have plenty of room and you could save all your money. I could baby sit for you." Bonnie sounded sober and seemed to have thought this through. Tilly thought it was a good offer, but she was skeptical.

"Mom, I can't move everything and give up my apartment only to be booted out every time Carl comes back," Tilly finally said.

"Carl's married," Bonnie said quickly.

"Oh, mom you didn't tell me...why didn't you tell me?"

"I...I...just couldn't. I got hurt so bad, but I'm okay now." Bonnie sounded as if she was going to cry.

"Mom, I'll think about it. I have to go, Cindy is at the door to baby sit for me to go to work. Everything will work out. Call ya tomorrow – bye." Tilly hung up the phone saddened by her conversation with her mom. She greeted Cindy, gave her instructions and jumped into her car. She would be late if she didn't hurry. She turned her radio on and sang as she went down the road. She thought about moving in with her mom. It would certainly help her situation right now. If she could handle this arrangement a little while, it would help save money. Sonny almost never gave her money and it was getting tight without Sis's help.

Tilly went in to work and went to the back room to put away her stuff. Diane came in and said something, but Tilly was deep in thought.

"Hey, what's wrong with you?" Diane asked, impatient with Tilly.

"Mom asked me to move in and she would help with Rae." Tilly turned around from hanging up her purse.

"You are not thinking of doing that are you? She will hurt you and will start in on Rae. If things are that bad, come back and live with me," Diane pleaded.

"No, the place is too small and Rae is everywhere. No, I can't do that to you, but I can take mom a while anyway until I can save some money. I'm about to lose my apartment and I can't keep up...I'm just tired," Tilly said wearily and reached for a cloth to wash tables.

"Oh, Til...I'm so sorry. I didn't know."

"Don't feel sorry for me now. I'll be fine."

"Sonny doesn't give you any money does he?" Diane asked, a little angry.

"Every now and then," Tilly said. Tilly went out to the counter to clean and knocked over the ketchup bottle. Ketchup went everywhere.

"Oh dear!" Tilly exclaimed.

"Go do something else, I got this," Diane said. Diane had not seen Tilly this down.

Tilly realized she would not be able to keep her apartment. She thought it would be hard when Sis moved out, but she did not think it would be impossible. She moved in with Bonnie despite her misgivings. Tilly told herself it would be temporary and she would save enough to get a place later.

It was a nice day to move and Sonny actually showed up with his truck to help. Tilly never knew what to expect from him, but she took all the help he offered.

"Just thought I would come and help ya'll move...well ya don't have to look at me with that look...I know that look now." Tilly was standing by her old comet looking at him as Sonny was getting out of his truck.

"Aren't you at least gonna speak? I don't think you know how to appreciate me. Here I am willing to help and not even a greeting," Sonny said. Tilly slammed the trunk to her brown comet.

"If you had paid child support, I wouldn't be moving," Tilly said as she brushed past him on her way back in the apartment.

"Hey, I did what I could. Business has been slow." Sonny threw up his arms and followed Tilly.

"Ya know, a little less drinking would have helped. How can you keep a business going when you are not there for the customers?" Tilly said scolding Sonny. She was mad at Sonny in more ways than one.

"Hey, I'm here now and I have money to give ya," Sonny said reaching for his wallet. Tilly looked at the cash Sonny had his hands and contemplated not taking it, but she quickly snatched it and put it in her old torn jeans. She told herself, it was for Rae.

She had to keep a cool head for Rae. She turned around and nodded.

"Grab those chairs, and you can carry the mattress!" She barked orders at Sonny and he complied.

Tilly was in her old room putting away her things and Bonnie was looking on smoking a cigarette. She had been helpful and especially good with Rae. Tilly did not want to hope this would last. She had to be realistic or she would be hurt. Rae was getting into everything Tilly pulled out and Tilly was getting short with her.

"Rae, why don't you and I go to the kitchen and find something good to eat. I bet I have some Oreo cookies and some milk," Bonnie said as she reached out to Rae.

"Where is Sonny?" Bonnie turned back around to ask Tilly.

"I don't know, he should be here by now. Who knows about Sonny? He has the mattress for this bed, I hope he gets here before tonight. I'm glad to have the help...but he is so...I don't know. He tries sometimes." Tilly went back to folding her clothes. Bonnie went on into the kitchen with Rae.

"Daddy!" Tilly heard Rae's voice. She must have seen her dad come in the driveway.

"Well it is about time," Tilly muttered to herself and went out the screen door to help get the mattress in. She jumped over the middle step and looked up when Sonny slammed the truck door hard.

"What now?" Tilly asked walking toward the truck. Sonny pointed to the mattress and Tilly went around to see what Sonny was upset about.

"Oh by the way, I hope you weren't too fond of that mattress. It blew off the truck and a lady ran right over it...just ran right over it and got stuck. That wasn't enough, she did a burnout getting off of it. Stupid!" Sonny threw up his arms. Tilly observed the stuffing coming out of the mattress and the springs popping out.

"Ya didn't tie it down Sonny!" Tilly yelled.

"Well who knew? I can tell you this much, it was heavy enough getting back into the truck.

Who would think it would blow off?" Sonny shot back.

"It should have been tied down. Haven't you seen all the mattress's on the side of the road? Well...?" Tilly challenged Sonny.

"Oh, like you know it all. I've had it!" Sonny took off his baseball cap and threw it down.

"Sonny this is so typical. Now I have to spend more money and get a mattress. Thanks for the help!" Tilly yelled again.

"It's not my fault. If that lady had not run over it, it would have been fine. I would have just picked it up and come on," Sonny was saying looking for an excuse. He did not like to feel stupid. Tilly turned around and stomped up on the porch. Bonnie was standing at the screen door with a cigarette in her hand. When Tilly brushed past her, Bonnie said. "Told ya something was missing up here with that one." She tapped her head.

"Oh mom, stop it!" Tilly continued past her.

Miss June was in the yard doing some gardening and had witnessed enough of the conversation to know what happened. She shook her head. She would go over later with some food, but she wanted Sonny to be gone. She had a good mattress in storage and she would offer it to Tilly.

When Tilly received the mattress from Miss June she was relieved. Sonny had almost cost her more to help move her than she had saved. That was the way it seemed to go in life for Sonny, always spinning his wheels and never accomplishing anything.

Tilly worried about the influence Bonnie might have on Rae. She was picking up some of her grandmother's bad habits. However, Bonnie had settled down a great deal and Tilly hoped this would last.

Sis was living in Florida with her boyfriend. They worked hourly wage jobs and barely made a living. Sis would call sometimes and that was all that she got from her. Bobby had quit school and was living with some friends. He worked when he needed to, and Tilly worried about him a lot more than her mom did.

Chapter 11

Spring 1983

Tilly had put a board over the middle loose step where Rae had often fallen. One day she would fix it right, but for now this would help. Rae was practicing toddling up and down and singing, "Old Macdonald Had a Farm." Tilly was observing her to see if her idea was working. Tilly had also painted the front porch gray with black shutters on the windows. She thought the whole look was coming together and was a great improvement. Things were going well with this move home. Tilly was peaceful for a change. She enjoyed her visits with Miss June and learned some gardening. They picked and prepared figs. The place was looking good and Tilly liked the yard work more than she had thought.

Tilly still enjoyed partying with her friends and had some wild nights. She would sometimes get restless and would take off for the evening. Tilly still could not settle too much, there was a restlessness about her and she did not know what it was. She dated some, but often felt lonely. Sometimes when she looked in the mirror she saw her mother's face looking back at her. She was getting older and she did not want to resemble her mom. Tilly thought if she could find someone decent to marry then maybe she would settle in her spirit. She didn't ask for much out of life, so why was this one thing so difficult. She did not want Rae raised the way she was being raised, and knew that the road she had taken was leading that way. Life was getting away from her.

"Going out again?" Bonnie asked in a grumpy way when Tilly was headed out the door one evening.

"Mom, don't start with me," Tilly shot back as a car horn blew outside.

"Ya know, you take me for granted," Bonnie said sitting like a cat on the couch, ready to pounce on Tilly.

"What is that suppose to mean?" Tilly asked turning around with a tone in her voice that made Bonnie back down. They both knew not to go further with this argument. Tilly had never forgiven her mother for her own lost childhood, and Bonnie knew that. Somehow in Tilly's now misguided mind, all this justified her behavior and lifestyle now. Bonnie, however, saw her mistakes and wanted better for Tilly. She knew she would not be able to tell Tilly anything. She watched as Tilly fixed her hair at the mirror on the wall beside the door. Bonnie leaned back in the old green

couch, faded with age, and sighed. She closed
her eyes and listened to the screen door creak
open and close.

Tilly's footfalls were fading out when Bonnie
opened her eyes. Rae was standing in front of
her holding a stuffed bear.

"Mommy gone again?" Rae asked sadly.

"Yes Rae, you need to get back in bed."
Bonnie took her hand and led her back to the
bedroom.

Chapter 12

Summer 1983

"So you are pregnant again." Bonnie was at the bathroom door confronting Tilly.

Tilly's helpless pale face looked up from the toilet bowl. She did not feel like this conversation right now. She got up, brushed past Bonnie and went to her room. She got her purse and said, "I'm late for work. Don't forget to drop off Rae at the day care center."

"I've only forgotten once. I don't know why you feel as if you have to remind me," Bonnie argued back, and Tilly turned around and gave her the look.

"Look, if you think I'm going to help raise another baby...well you can forget it!" Bonnie was pointing at Tilly and yelling.

Tilly walked out and tried to fall down the steps. She was blindly mad and upset with wild thoughts. She opened the car door, got in, took a deep breath and cranked the car. Maybe she would have an accident on the way to work. She peeled out of the driveway, but slowed down when Rae's face appeared in her mind. A sweet angel who loved her unquestionably, how could she have such thoughts? Her mind went to the scene last night. Hank, nicknamed Red because of his red hair and his fiery temper, had asked her to marry him. She did not love him, and she knew he probably did not love her. She was thinking now that she had no choice, she could not depend upon her mom.

She remembered when she had met Red a few months earlier. He was big, over six feet tall. He had staggered over to her while she was at the bar she frequented. She was playing pool and had actually made a good shot. He swigged his beer and winked at her.

"Good shot," he said as Tilly looked up.

"Can I buy you a drink?" he continued.

"Sure," she replied.

Red began to win her over with his protectiveness. He could be charming, telling her she was beautiful and wonderful. She was hooked for a while. Now he was her fate.

Tilly was married in a simple ceremony at a chapel near her home. Rae strolled down the small aisle with her white basket of rose petals, dropping them lightly as she walked. Her blonde hair was curled for the occasion and her blue eyes were opened wide looking at the crowd. She was more curious about what was happening than anything else, because she liked the attention. Rae knew her little life was changing, but could not grasp just how.

Tilly and Red had a short honeymoon in Florida before settling in a home life. Rae, with much protest, stayed with her grandmother for a few weeks to allow Tilly and Red some time alone and to start their home together.

Tilly gave birth to twin boys five months later. They came as fast as Rae had, and Tilly had made sure she got to the hospital quickly. They were not identical; it was evident from the beginning. The small bundle that came first with the already reddish hair was named Hank Jr. A couple of minutes later a little white-haired boy came, and they called him Matthew. From the start, they were a hand-full.

Chapter 13

1984-90

Red made money in the trucking business and they moved out in the country in a small farm house. Red was on the road in his truck most of the time and this suited Tilly. The solitary life was, at first, great and then with time Tilly became restless. She was glad Red was on the road more than he was home because she had come to realize he had quite a temper. She had not known Red well enough before she married him, and even regretted the decision she had made. She never would have aborted her twins, but if she had known about Red, she would have gone it on her own. She dreaded when he came home, and at the same time longed for him to help her with her daily tasks.

Time went by as slowly as a hot summer day. Tilly came to know Red's personality more, and realized he was a control freak. He had moved her in the middle of nowhere to make sure that she lost all ties to friends and home. She had no job to make her own money and totally had to depend on Red. He gave her only a certain amount of money for food and gas. This did not allow her enough for trips home, or many trips other than to the small grocery. Tilly thought she would lose her mind. He took to knocking her around when she protested her meager existence. When she stopped fussing about her conditions, he still found reasons to hit and yell at her. Tilly wanted to leave and started plotting. She knew Red was capable of anything, and she knew she had to be careful. She did not want Rae living like this or give him the opportunity to start hitting her. Rae had bucked him a couple of times and he started for her, but Tilly got Rae out of his way and smoothed things over. She couldn't keep this up. When Red came off a long trip one evening, he provided Tilly with the push she needed to leave.

"Ya know ya should feel lucky I married you," Red stated after they had argued over dinner. He stood up and went to the refrigerator to get a beer.

"Yeah, I'm real lucky," Tilly said sarcastically.

"Girl, you are about to get it," Red said as he slammed the refrigerator door.

"Oh yeah, hit me, go ahead! That is what you want to do!" Tilly stood toe to toe with him and her hands clutched. Rae started weeping.

"You are just a spoiled rotten brat and you think you have to have it all. You don't have to work. You have food and a roof over your head. What more do you want?" Red was getting angrier, and took a big swig of beer. Tilly got in his face.

"You moved me out here in the sticks you big bully. You control every thing and I get nothing but what you allow. If you could control the air I breathe, you would, and believe me I wouldn't get much of that either! I like to work and I like to see people!" Tilly yelled. Red pushed her away from him and Rae was crying louder. The twins woke up and began crying.

"Ya don't need to work. I don't know why you're not happy! You know, I'm tired of you and I have a long trip tomorrow." Red brushed past Rae's chair and headed toward the bedroom. "Would you stop these kids from crying?" He yelled back.

After that night, Tilly made trips back home to see her mom and friends. She would stay longer periods of time each trip she made. Red, for whatever reason, gave her the money to do this. Perhaps he saw this to be easier to deal with than keeping her cooped up so that she blew up when he got home.

One weekend Tilly left with the intention of not going back. Red, however, sweet-talked her into going back with many promises. For years this was the pattern of living for those two. Tilly partied when Red left for extended trucking trips, and she got away with a lot. As things have a way of happening, Red found out about some things, and one day beat her within an inch of her life. He beat on her to rid himself of whatever torment he was living. Ten-year-old Rae and the five-year-old boys looked on this for the last time before things would really change for them.

Tilly waited for Red to leave two weeks later on a long trip. She had healed some. She packed everything and left Red for good. The kids knew. Hank Jr. wiped tears flowing down his face as he sat in the car. Matthew looked scared, and Rae was happy.

Tilly arrived home and Bonnie came out to greet them. Bobby was sitting on the front porch. Tilly had called to let her mom know she was coming for good; however the presence of Bobby surprised her. When her mom was hugging the kids at the car Tilly spoke, "Bobby's home again, I see."

"Ya know that ole gal he was with..." and she muttered something Tilly did not pick up on. The kids started running around the yard, getting out all of their energy. They climbed the fig tree. Tilly walked up to the porch and observed that the middle step still had not been fixed.

"When is someone going to fix this thing?" Tilly looked at Bobby.

"Hey, Til." Bobby waved his hand, but pretended not to hear about the step.

"I'll have to get a board and put across it again or the kids will fall for sure," Tilly said hoping Bobby would say something, but he didn't.

"Heard from Sis," Bonnie said as they walked in carrying things. The kids were hitting each other and Tilly yelled at them. She turned to her mother.

"Is she all right?" Tilly asked.

"Yeah, she said she was getting married," Bonnie said wearily. Tilly nodded, she knew this wasn't a good match from what she had heard.

"So, Bobby, what is your plan for the future?" Tilly turned around when Bobby walked in with some of her stuff.

"I might go to tech school," He said.

"That's good," Tilly replied.

"Well, I've got supper fixed so let's go eat before it gets cold," Bonnie said.

When they had eaten and cleaned up the kitchen, the twins and Rae were put to bed. They were tired from the trip and fell asleep fast. Bobby went back outside in the spring evening. He liked to sit outside. Bonnie and Tilly were left alone.

"Well, you are getting older. What are your plans?" Bonnie asked digging at Tilly.

"Mom, stop aging me. I don't know what I am going to do. I just knew we had to leave," Tilly said and yawned.

"I hope for good this time. I talked to Billy and he wants you back," Bonnie said.

Tilly did not respond. She was too tired to think of that.

"Ya know, I've stopped drinking. I can't give up those cigarettes though, but I'm trying to," Bonnie said.

"Oh mom that is great. I thought something was different. You seem at peace," Tilly said and smiled. Bonnie got up to fix coffee. When she came back she sat down on the sofa across from Tilly.

"Do you...think I could be... forgiven by you and the other kids...ever?" Bonnie asked pitifully. Tilly got up and hugged her.

"Mom, I know what you went through...I'm not perfect. I've made my own mistakes with my kids to tell you anything. I need a big change too. Maybe I will go get my old job back and go to the Jr. College," Tilly said with some hope.

Bonnie put her hands on Tilly's hands and said, "Stay as long as you need to."

Chapter 14

1990-94

Tilly and her mom had some healing time during this move home. Things were good and Bonnie's health improved somewhat due to her giving up drinking and most of her cigarette smoking. Bonnie went to church often, and Tilly and the kids went every now and then. The kids were adjusting to school, but the area was growing at a rapid rate and Tilly worried about her kids' progress in the schools. She made a hard decision and moved farther out. Leaving her mom concerned her because she felt she needed to be with her as she got older, and Bonnie was attached to the children.

Bobby had moved back in to stay for a while, and he seemed to be helping more around the house. He was enrolled at the technical school and he was going to rehab for help. Tilly felt he could handle things around the house and he got along with Bonnie well. It was this situation that gave Tilly the go-ahead to move. Bonnie encouraged her to do what was best for the kids.

Tilly found a trailer outside of town that would serve until she could do better. She could fix it up. She was ashamed of the location of it - next to the dump. The boys loved it and scurried through the junk often. Boys and junkyards seem to go together. Tilly thought there could be worse things in life and left them to this activity. It took up time and kept them out of trouble. Rae was a different story as she approached those teen-age years. Tilly would have her hands full with her.

Tilly continued working at Billy's. It was a long drive and she made the best of it by singing as she drove down the road. In 1992 she enrolled in the Jr. College and decided to take classes toward a nursing degree. This was a hard schedule for a mother of three. She could have used some help. Sonny offered to help, but Sonny had not changed and was not reliable. Sonny had been in and out of Rae's life when he felt like it. The emotional problems this caused Rae could have only been a guess.

Red was another story. He had never accepted Tilly's leaving him and had attempted many reconciliations. When the final divorce papers went through despite him, he was angrier than ever. He came to see the boys some in between road trips. He could not keep them for long periods of time due to his time on the road. Tilly felt bad that the boys could not be with their father, but the decision she made was for the best.

One evening after several years at "the dump" as they fondly called their humble abode, Tilly was once again getting ready for work. Tilly was in a pretty good mood after passing an important test, so she did not let anything bother her right now. She wouldn't even let having to work the late shift this evening get her down. When she walked through the small messy trailer, she dreamed of a house she could buy. She frequently went through the realty books and circled houses. She kept her mind on a goal and overlooked the number of hardships. The interest rates were still high after the recession, but Tilly knew she had a chance when things got better. She gathered up her things and went to find the boys outside. Rae was spending a rare week with Sonny. She did not know what brought this on. School was almost out for the summer, and Tilly tried to tell him that he needed to get Rae to school every morning. It was a long drive for him and she doubted he would be consistent. She thought about not letting him get Rae, and would have talked to him about it, but Rae ran out the door with her stuff and got in the car when Sonny drove up. The two of them were hard to deal with together, and all she could do was tell both of them about the importance of school. She had to let it go right now and get to work. She walked around the trailer.

"Boys, get inside...now!" Tilly yelled. She walked back in to get her purse. It was warm inside. She got the pliers that were on the floor and turned the broken knob on the fan. The boys had managed to break off the plastic button that enclosed the metal pin that was left. She shook her head and thought nothing was safe around them.

The evening shift was hard when Rae wasn't there to help. Rae, at fourteen, was a pretty good babysitter for the boys. She liked to be the boss. The twins were ten, and were growing fast. She didn't like to leave the boys alone and had tried to get a neighbor to help this evening. She was unsuccessful at the last minute and had to make the best of the situation. Tilly hoped when she got out of school that she would have a "normal" life for her children. That is what she held on to in times like these to keep away the guilt that loved to grab her tightly.

"Ya'll get in here now! You have homework to do, and no T.V. Your food is on the counter and...bed early. Mrs. Lee is going to check on you when she gets home." Tilly was barking orders over the strong protests of the boys as they came around the trailer. Tilly tussled the blond and red haired boys as they passed her going through the door. Tilly heard the blast of the T.V. before she got to her old brown Comet. She turned around and yelled, "T.V. off!" She heard silence and was satisfied. She opened the old creaky door. The car had been hit on that door and it was hard to open and close. Tilly did not notice this old door anymore, she was used to it and slammed it hard when she got in behind the wheel. She cranked the car and turned on the radio - loud. She loved the music loud and her favorite song was on. She beat time to the music with the window down and her curly blond hair blowing. She popped some gum into her mouth and continued to sing loudly. The back broken bumper was flopping up and down on the pot-holed road. It was hitting the pavement every now and again, and Tilly continued down the road singing, paying no attention to the noise she made. It took thirty minutes to get to work, and sometimes Tilly regretted moving that far out. However, she enjoyed the solitude the drive offered. She let her hair down during this time.

Tilly pulled into Billy's. She was surprised to see cars in the parking lot. This time of the evening was usually very slow. Customers usually came later for dinner and earlier for lunch. She was hoping for some time to get some things done before waiting tables. Occasionally "Uncle Joe" as they all called him was here at this time. He liked to come in when there were no customers. Tilly wondered if he was in his usual seat, and she was thinking about him as she gathered up her purse and got out of the car. She saw "Uncle Joe" in the window and waved, and he smiled his toothless smile. He lived in an old shack down the road; and rumor had it that he kept money under his mattress. She pondered on that a moment and laughed to herself, wondering if that could be so as she approached the door. A funny feeling came over her as she opened the door. The bell over the door dinged as she walked into the cafe. She shook off the funny feeling when she turned around to close the door. It had a habit of sticking open. Satisfied with the door she turned around to see Diane looking at her and filling up the ketchup bottles. She motioned excitedly to Tilly to come over.

"Look whose here!" Diane pointed to the two men at the corner table by the wall. Tilly looked over and saw Preacher James Bell facing her, and she could only see the back of another man's head. She shook her head questioningly at Diane. Diane looked over at the men.

"Oh, you can't see the other man. Go give the Smiths some water, and when you turn around take a quick look without calling attention to yourself," Diane said and handed the water pitcher to her. Tilly forgot to take out her gum, and as carefree as ever walked over to the couple by the window. Preacher James and the stranger had observed Tilly as she walked across the floor. Tilly was very attractive and caught the eyes of most men in a room, even though she never seemed to be aware of this fact. The stranger took in a lot during a minute of watching Tilly. He noticed her nice blonde hair and big hazel eyes. She had a nice figure and a sassy walk. She was clicking her gum as she walked, and the soles of shoes unattached to the tops flopped up and down like flip flops instead of shoes. He found this amusing as he continued to watch her because she seemed unaware of the condition of her shoes. That is what made it even funnier to him. She was a happy sort, and carefree. He saw a lot in the seconds he had observed this woman. He was curious and he felt life took a whole new meaning for him in a matter of seconds.

Tilly turned around and looked straight into his eyes. Her jaw dropped and she was completely immobile. She was staring at the man of her dreams, the only man she had ever had a crush on in her entire life! Here he was, bigger than life. Their eyes locked. Diane came over and aroused her out of her trance and pushed Tilly's mouth closed.

"Get a grip, girl," Diane whispered as she led Tilly back to the counter.

"But it's..." Tilly was stammering.

"I know...I know...lets just walk behind the counter." Diane continued to guide Tilly, and Tilly was straining to still keep her eyes on her man. He had an amused look on his face as he turned and watched the girls. Diane took the pitcher of water before Tilly dropped it.

"Is that really him? Of course it is...there is only one man like that." Tilly was stammering.

"It is him in the flesh. Can you believe it? It seems he is an old childhood friend of Preacher James. Funny he never mentioned that," Diane said with her hand on her hips.

"How would you know if he had mentioned it? It's not like you are at church to find out anything," Tilly said.

"Well, it just seems that would have come out...you know...sometime. Well it seems he is here to speak this week at the revival. It might be time to go to church...anyway he made some sort of change a few years ago and well...that's all I know," Diane said quickly.

"Oh my!" Diane exclaimed.

"What...what is the matter?" Tilly asked.

"I have not taken their order. You go. I can't." Diane pushed Tilly toward them and handed her an order pad. "Go!" Diane ordered when Tilly hesitated. Tilly slowly walked to the table and took a deep breath.

"Uh, may I take your order? My name is Tilly...I'm Tilly. Are you ready to order?" Tilly had her pad ready and broke the pencil point on it. She reached in her pocket for another pencil.

"Hello Tilly. Haven't seen you in church in a while," Preacher James greeted her. "This is Tim Reynolds, a friend from...well way back. Tim this is Tilly...Uh... what is your last name now?" Preacher James asked.

"Oh, I went back to Morgan legally... it was better that way. How do you do," Tilly quickly wiped her hands on the cloth hanging from her belt and shook Tim's hand.

"I've probably seen every movie you have made," Tilly said and took their order. She rolled her eyes on the way back to the kitchen. She had acted like a complete idiot.

Billy had observed the whole scene.

"Well, give me the order girl," Billy said. Tilly was just staring into space. Billy reached over and took the order out of her hand. He had never seen Tilly speechless. Tim was still looking toward the direction of the women and Billy. He turned back and grinned at his friend with a curious look on his face.

"So what's her story?" Tim asked, not sure he wanted to know. He could not explain why his heart had jumped at the sight of her, and he needed information.

"She's a mess, married a couple of times, drinks, smokes and parties. When I became the preacher here a few years ago, when I was young, I thought I could save everybody. Her family was one I was determined to help. Tilly was fifteen and wild then. Her mom had men in and out of their lives. The other two kids were messed up too. Tilly ran away a couple of times, finally the inevitable happened. I think she is good at heart, means well and all, but couldn't get herself out of the web. Her mother made a change a few years back and attends church. She stopped drinking...I don't think she gave up smoking though. She sees her way now, and has asked prayers for her children. I heard that Tilly is going to college and is trying to do better. We'll see." Preacher James shook his head as he wrapped up Tilly's story.

"Well, she may need someone to help her, you know, like a friend from church. Visiting her might help now. Look at me, I'm over forty and am now changed. It's never too late," Tim said still contemplating the fascinating creature walking around the small café. What was it about her that made him want to know more?

"She lives farther out now. We tried a couple of times to visit and the kids were home alone," Preacher James said.

Tilly came back to the table a little more composed. She gave them the iced tea they had ordered.

"I hope you like real sweet tea," Tilly timidly said.

"You know I do," Preacher James spoke up.

"Well the South wouldn't be the South without nice ice cold sweet tea, and the sweeter the better." With that said, Tim winked at Tilly, raised his glass and started drinking his tea. Tilly froze for second and nervously laughed. She dreamily walked back to Diane. Diane was wringing her hands and biting her lower lip.

"Well what did he say?" Diane asked shaking Tilly's arm.

"Why don't you take the salad over Diane? It's not fair that I should have all the fun," Tilly told Diane. Billy was watching everything with interest. When Tilly went back to the kitchen to retrieve the salads, Billy was standing there with his arms crossed.

"I heard he was a widower," he said.

"Who?" Tilly asked still not really paying attention. Billy nodded out toward the tables and he was chewing on a toothpick.

"Cancer," he stated.

"What?" Tilly asked still busy with the salads.

"His wife died a few months ago from cancer," Billy continued.

"Goodness, I didn't know that. I wonder why I didn't hear about that. That's bad...they were married for so long," Tilly said sadly. Tilly had been so busy with work and school that she had missed the news. She had admired this man so long, and one of the reasons was because of his devotion to his wife and family. They were the examples of what marriage could be, and what Tilly wanted and longed for. Diane was busy with other customers so Tilly took the salads to the table.

"It's getting busy now," Preacher James observed.

"Yes, it is our busy time now. Your order should be coming in a few minutes," Tilly said and started to walk away. Tim took something out of his pocket and handed it to Tilly. It was a flier from church.

"Here, why don't you come to church Sunday night? I'll be speaking," Tim was saying as Tilly took the paper from him.

"I'm real sorry about your wife...I just heard about it." Tilly stumbled for words.

"Thank you for your concern...it's been hard. I've found comfort in the Lord now. She was a good Christian woman and a good mother," Tim replied sadly. Tilly nodded and left the table. Diane was keeping an eye on the scene.

"What did he give you?" Diane asked when they again met behind the counter.

"It's a church brochure about the revival," Tilly answered, and Diane rolled her eyes. "Preacher James has been handing those out for a while," Diane said.

"Did you look at it?" Tilly asked.

"No...I wasn't gonna go hear about how bad I am. I already know that," Diane shot back and laughed.

"It says Tim Reynolds would be speaking. How did we miss this?" Tilly was talking to herself because Diane had walked away.

The night became busy and Tilly waited on other tables while trying to get over to Tim as often as possible. They stayed and talked over dessert and coffee for a long time. When they left, Tilly felt empty. She could not explain this feeling. As a teenager Tilly had plastered her room with Tim's images. She had kept all the ticket stubs to his movies. He still looked the same except better, in her opinion. His blond hair had gray through it, but his blue eyes were as blue as ever. Age had made him even more handsome. She would not have guessed Preacher James was Tim's same age. Preacher James had seemed so much older. He was balding and getting rounder with age. She remembered him as a teenager and thought he was always old. Now that Tilly was in her early thirties, they didn't seem so much older to her. She was thinking on all this when she realized Diane was talking to her.

"Wow, how many days would we have like this one...uh?" Diane elbowed Tilly.

"Uh...yeah...I know. Wait til I tell the kids," Tilly replied.

"Just think, we met a real star. He still looks good. He must be close to fifty," Diane said.

"Not quite," Tilly stated.

"Not quite what?" Diane asked confused.

"He is not fifty...yet, he is only ten years older than me," Tilly answered.

"Oh, so you know all about him...aren't you something," Diane responded, and looked up to see Billy giving them the look. They quickly got busy.

Tilly got home that evening feeling pretty happy, she had sung all the way home. When she walked into the small trailer, Rae was standing there. Her fourteen-year-old looked twenty-one, and was made up like a street walker.

Rae what are you doing here? You were supposed to stay with your dad through the weekend." Tilly caught herself from saying anything further. There was a lot to say and she wanted to grab her, but Rae's stance was like a deer ready to run. Tilly had to be sneaky.

"Dad's so...you know..." Rae shrugged.

"Dad is a little hard on you...uh...wh...where did you get those clothes?" Tilly asked trying to keep herself composed. She put her hand to her forehead, there was a headache coming on. Tilly geared up. She would have to be strong as tired as she was.

"Rae, you know how I feel about all the make-up and those clothes..."

"No...No...Mom don't start up with me...Dad tried this too!" Rae threw her hand up in front of her mom.

"Look, I don't want to argue tonight. I have a test Monday and I need to start a paper. I have to work breakfast shift...so let's drop it and you go on to bed," Tilly said wearily.

"Mom, you always have school work. How long can a person go to school, you've been in school all my life!" Rae shot back and put her hand on her hips.

"You know I've been working for my nurse's degree. It takes years to do it the way I've had to do it. When I get out, it will pay off. This is what happens when you cut your young life off, and the opportunities that come along with it," Tilly lectured not wanting to give this moment up to make a point. Rae rolled her eyes.

"Oh, by the way, we are going to church Sunday morning and evening," Tilly was saying to Rae as Rae was stomping down the hall to her room.

"Mom, church? Oh please, get real! Christmas and Easter are enough times to go to church," Rae jerked around and yelled.

"That is enough Rae, go to bed," Tilly said as she took the pliers to turn the fan up. Rae made her final statement by slamming the door. Tilly turned the fan toward the table where she would have to work for an hour or so. She went to check on the boys and came back to settle in to work on her paper. She tried to keep her mind on what she should be doing, but a pair of gorgeous blue eyes kept popping in front of her mind. His smile made her melt and his laugh rang in her ears over and over again. The crush she had had on him years ago had not faded. Her dream of meeting him had actually come true and she could not wait until Sunday. Rae would not know who he was, or care, so to explain why they were making an extra trip to church would have been futile. She shook herself of her dreaming, she had to work now. She must carry on no matter what, now was not the time to mess up.

She was busy working on her books when she heard a car on the gravel drive. She wondered why it stopped down the drive. She took off her reading glasses and pulled the curtain open. She quickly turned out the light to see. The car was at the end of the drive. They turned the car lights off and sat there. She heard something in the back of the trailer. It sounded like a window opening. She was frightened for a second until a figure came running around the corner from the back. Tilly jerked the curtain closed and stalked out the door. Rae looked back and started running toward the car.

"Rae, you get back in this house now!" Tilly yelled as she took off after her daughter. Tilly caught her shirt and Rae was struggling.

"Get inside now!" Tilly was holding on tightly, and while they tussled the car skidded off.

"Now look what you did! I am not a baby. You can't treat me this way!" Rae yelled and ran into the trailer. Tilly heard Rae's bedroom door slam when she got inside.

What was she going to do now? That had been a close call. She would have to interrogate Rae another day to get to the bottom of this incident. Sonny would be no help, he either was too hard on her or he gave up and let her be. He let her skip too many days at school, because to get her up and listen to her fuss was something he did not want to deal with. Tilly needed help. She would call Miss June. Miss June would calm her down. She knew how to pray, and Tilly wished she knew how to pray like Miss June. She concentrated again on her studies with a good thought of Sunday coming up.

After work on Saturday morning, Tilly begged off the lunch shift to get home to Rae. She knew she had slept late and would be getting up. She had lectured Rae and grounded her for quite a while. She was in the middle of the argument with Rae when Red called up. He was drunk, and when he was drunk sometimes he called Tilly and harassed her. She had gotten a restraining order against him earlier and that just made him angrier. Tilly felt overwhelmed and needed Sunday morning to get here fast. She had promised Billy to work the Sunday breakfast shift in exchange for Saturday afternoon. She would miss the early church service, but she would surly make it to the evening service.

She knew Tim would be speaking only in the evening, so this did not bother her too much.

Tilly wanted to arrive at Billy's early Sunday. Billy opened early for the breakfast crowd that came before church, and stayed open until the lunchtime church crowd. He closed on Sunday evening only. Billy often went on to church after the early crowd left if it looked like he could leave. He sometimes offered to let Tilly and Diane go if they wanted to and he would stay, but they always turned him down. Tilly was eager to work today. Tilly was driving down the road thinking about things, with the music on high and she was singing. Yes, she was looking forward to the evening service. She was tired of Rae's whining and hoped she would not have trouble with her tonight. She had gotten to the point that if she heard "it's not fair" one more time, she would slap Rae. She knew Rae would probably slap her back, so she had to stay calm even with Rae's smart mouth.

Tilly turned into Billy's with her music loud and her windows down. Her blond hair was ruffled. She looked in the rear view mirror to straighten her hair and check her make-up, when lights caught her eye. She turned down the radio and heard a quick siren. Tilly rolled her eyes and put her head on the steering wheel.

"Til, what have I said to you before?" It was Rob Hardy, a guy Tilly dated some in high school, now turned policeman. "I'm afraid I'm going to have to write a ticket this time Tilly. You've been warned too many times. Not only that, I've been trying to get your attention for a while. I've been following you since Willow Street. You need to slow it down, that's all there is to it." Rob was looking in the window speaking.

"Oh officer, this young lady will slow down next time, she seems harmless enough." A man's voice spoke and before Tilly lifted her head, she knew the voice because she had heard it a thousand times, and it even echoed in her dreams. When she looked up, Tim was standing there grinning from ear to ear. That smile and those blue eyes, right in front of her, and she couldn't get any words out.

"Oh wow! Tim Reynolds! I've been a fan of yours for years...uh...I heard you were in town. Hey...could I have your autograph?" Rob was getting something for him to write on and Tim gave Tilly a wink. Tim complied with the request and Rob turned to Tilly.

"Uh...oh...Til...you can have another chance, but next time..."

"Yeah, thanks Rob. I'll slow down next time, I promise," Tilly said and waved at him as he walked off. He tipped his hat and left. When he got to his car, he turned around and said to Tim, "Thanks for the autograph, if I weren't on duty this evening, I would have liked to come to service tonight. Hope it goes well, see ya'll later." When he drove off Tim turned around laughing.

"What's so funny?" Tilly asked.

"The look on your face, like a scared, cornered rabbit," Tim laughingly replied.

"Thanks for getting me off., I didn't need a ticket right now," she said getting out of the car. She shut the door and Tim reached around her to attempt to close the door better. She held her breath for a moment with the closeness of him, and then she could smell him. He smelled good too, just like she had imagined he would. He gave the door a shove but it did not shut.

"The door won't shut, it's stuck," Tim said.

"Yeah...well...you have ta kick it." With that said, Tilly turned around and kicked the door shut. It clicked. She turned back around to see Tim trying not to laugh.

"It's an old car...well you can see that," Tilly said and laughed and they both went in the café laughing.

Billy and Diane had seen the exchange outside through the window. The police lights had caught their attention. When Tilly and Tim started in, Diane and Billy quickly got busy. Tim had opened the door for Tilly. Diane was cleaning the counter and Billy was at the grill, both acting as if they had seen nothing.

"Hey Til - Mr. Reynolds," Diane greeted them.

"Call me Tim, please," Tim said and stuck out his hand to Diane. Diane took his hand and dreamily looked Tim in the eyes.

"Did you see Rob catch me again?" Tilly interrupted.

"Oh Tilly, you are going to get a big fat ticket one day," Diane said, but she was still gazing at Tim.

"Maybe she has learned her lesson this time," Tim said. There was a silent moment.

"Tim, I'll show you to a table and take your order when you're ready." Tilly broke the silence. When she had settled Tim at a table with some water and coffee, she went back to the small break room. Billy had made a space for them to get away from the dining area for breaks. It was no bigger than a closet, but Billy had squeezed a table and chairs in the area that used to be just a storage room. Tilly was putting away her purse when Billy stuck his head in.

"Everything all right?" Billy asked.

"Sure, sorry about being late. I was trying to be early...but time just got away...sorry," Tilly answered.

"Don't worry. I don't want you speeding to get here from now on," Billy said as he walked off. Tilly rolled her eyes, knowing Billy had seen what had happened. When Tilly walked out to the tables, Diane was already at Tim's table pouring him more coffee. Jealousy crept in, and she quickly went to the table.

"Would you like the special?" Tilly asked.

"Yes, that would be nice," Tim answered. Diane gave her a look as she passed Tilly.

"You are here early, you must be planning on going on to church. Are you speaking this morning?" Tilly said.

"No, I'm not speaking this morning, but I was going to go," Tim replied.

"I'll get your food quick enough so you will have plenty of time," Tilly said.

"Why are you giving me the evil eye?" Tilly asked Diane when she realized Diane was looking at her.

"You are hogging him, but he likes you," Diane responded.

"A movie star? Liking me? Sure." Tilly said sarcastically.

"I just wonder why Preacher James never mentioned this," Diane said.

"Like I said before, you would not have known what he said at church when you were not there. Besides we don't exactly hang around the church crowd," Tilly said as she got the order ready. She walked over and gave Tim his order, and felt he was observing her. He was still so handsome, she thought to herself. She turned around to wipe a table, and the crowd was starting to filter in. Some were going to church and took the easy special of two eggs, bacon and sausage. Tilly was quite busy the rest of the shift and missed talking much more to Tim.

Tilly was gathering up her things in the back room. She was tired and sat down for a moment.

"You still going this evening?" Diane asked when she saw Tilly's condition.

"Yes, I'm going home to fix lunch, rest for a while and gather the kids up to come back. I'm tired and it will take energy to drive back, but it will be worth it," Tilly said wearily. "What about you?"

"I don't think so...I might have a date," Diane answered.

"You are going to miss the biggest event in town...for a date? Diane, everyone is going!" Tilly exclaimed.

"Not everyone is going," Diane replied.

"Who are you going out with that isn't going?" Tilly asked and suddenly thought of something Rae had said in the middle of a heated argument. She had dismissed it then, but now looked at Diane closely. Diane was fidgeting.

"Sonny...you are going out with Sonny," Tilly said amazed at this revelation.

"Well, he is not still yours," Diane shot back.

"Sonny is not a person you want to deal with Diane, he can't be trusted," Tilly said, concerned.

"He has changed some, he is settling," Diane said.

"Well you are older than me; perhaps that is what he needs." Tilly couldn't resist the dig. Diane put her hands on her waist.

"Now Tilly, I know this is awkward. It just happened. I don't want to hurt you," Diane pleaded. Tilly was laughing to herself.

"What is so funny?" Diane asked, exasperated with Tilly.

"Punishment enough would be for you to be Rae's step-mother. Think about it," Tilly said as she picked up her purse and brushed past Diane. She waved at Diane before she went out the door. Diane stood stunned.

"Oh, no," Diane said to herself.

Tilly carefully put on as much make-up as she could. She fixed her mid-length hair even fluffier than usual. She had a time with Rae, but finally convinced her to get ready. The boys were ready and watching T.V. Tilly looked at the time on the bathroom clock and quickly finished. She knocked on Rae's door and yelled, "Let's go! Rae, turn off that music and let's get going!" Rae opened the door abruptly and startled Tilly.

"What?" Rae yelled over the music. Rae looked worse now than she did when she went to get ready. Tilly eyed her. Rae had changed her jeans, put on a tank and lots of jewelry. Her hair was sticking out everywhere with strange colors in it. She had on black lipstick and nails; and to top it off, black, thick, eye make-up. Hank Jr. and Matt were behind Tilly, looking. They were hoping for a fight.

"Are you going to a funeral?" Matt asked Rae, looking at the black tank and black jeans. Tilly held her breath hoping Rae would not attack her brother.

"I'm going like this...or not at all!" Rae yelled challenging her opponents. Tilly let her breath out and nodded. She was not going to argue.

"Let's get in the car," Tilly said, unaware that her own attire wasn't really appropriate for church either. She was trying to do something with the boys' hair, but they needed a haircut. She had not had the time to do even that.

Entering the church, Tilly and the kids immediately went for the back bench. Rae sat down and crossed her arms while rolling her eyes.

"Do we have to stay?" Rae asked, looking around and realizing she was out of place. Tilly smiled and waved to Miss June. She was up front and had noticed their arrival, along with most everyone else. This place brought back memories of the times she went to Vacation Bible School for so many summers with Miss June. Rae had attended when she was younger and the boys still came every summer.

"Can we sit with Miss June?" Hank asked Tilly. She looked up to where Miss June was sitting and there would be no room for all of them. Miss June was coming back to them.

"Let me take Hank and Matt up front with me," Miss June said to Tilly.

"All right." Tilly was thankful because that gave Rae and her more room in the crowded small church. It wasn't used to holding this many people. Tilly was sitting at the end toward the middle isle. She had a clear shot of Tim. She could not have been happier. She knew he would soon leave town and forget her, and she took every moment she could to watch him. The music was nice and Tilly joined in. Rae punched her arm. She ignored Rae and sang on. She did not care what Rae thought or did right now, she was going to enjoy this moment.

When the music stopped, Preacher James introduced Tim as a childhood friend who had recently made a change and looked him up after many years. It seems they had gone their separate ways and came back together as friends again. They had more in common now and Tim had reached out to his friend James for help with the mission work he was doing now. Tim had been to parts of Africa and had a calling to go back, and he wanted churches to back him in his work there.

Preacher James mentioned that he had prayed for Tim for years and was burdened about the lifestyle Tim had chosen. When Tim called, Preacher James dropped everything to talk with him many times on the phone. Tim had told him of his experience with the Lord and that he was ready for changes. He was losing his wife to cancer and he asked for prayer. Now, Tim was going to testify about how he came to know the Lord after so many years.

Tim spoke about the worldly pleasures he had partaken of and the wild living he had done. He also spoke about his wife's faith and faithfulness. He said she was the reason he was still alive and the reason he became a Christian. She had been the one to pray for him when he was out all night drinking and partying. He had been unfaithful in the marriage and still she forgave him. She had been a rock and he counted on her. When she got sick his world came apart and he sought help. He had talked to a great man of God, and everything began to make sense to him. He said we are all here for a purpose. He had a purpose and so did everyone. Rae squirmed, and Tilly dropped her eyes. She realized her fake eyelashes were loose so she took them off discreetly. Tim was talking, and at times his eyes fell on Tilly in the back. He continued to talk about the loose living in Hollywood and he looked back at Tilly. He noticed something different about her, but kept talking. He was on the subject of needing godly men and women in the country when he saw Tilly wiping her face. She was unaware she was being watched by Tim, and when she looked up she caught his eyes. Tim looked at her strangely because he noticed she was pale, having taken off all her make-up including the bright lipstick. He talked about his godly wife and how she had lived her life. She had made a difference in people's lives. He had not appreciated her and now felt the loneliness. Tilly was knotting her hair in a bun on her head, she did not want to appear like a worldly woman. Rae stared at her. Tim looked back at Tilly again and realized she had completely transformed before his eyes. He almost laughed, but thanked God inwardly because perhaps she was getting it.

The sermon was over and an invitation was given to come forward for prayer. Tilly became restless and wondered what was going on. She couldn't stand it any longer, so she buttoned the top button of her blouse and ran down the aisle. It wasn't for Tim that she ran down that aisle, she wouldn't do this for any person. No, this was real, this was God talking to her. She fell at the alter, she had got it. She knew she needed to change. A woman came over to pray with her and she felt someone behind her. It was Rae. Her face was streaked from the make-up and tears. "Mom," is all Rae said. Tim spoke to Tilly briefly, but others were needing his attention too. That was all right with Tilly, because she finally felt at peace. Miss June was rejoicing too because she had prayed for Tilly and her family for so long.

The drive home that evening was silent. They were deep in thought. Tilly could not realize that this would not be the end of her battles. It would be the beginning of new battles, hard and impossible battles for her to handle alone. She would have to learn to lean on the Lord. Rae would have her own battles ahead. Being a part of the crowd was easy, but to be different is hard. They would have their downfalls again and again, but they knew where their true strength came from.

Chapter 15

1995

"I heard you were moving back in with your mother," Diane said to Tilly one morning as they were starting the breakfast shift. Diane had noticed a change in Tilly and knew through the grape vine why. She had "got religion" was the phrase Sonny had used. Sonny and Diane weren't sure they liked the new Tilly. Diane felt Tilly had abandoned her and she looked for other friends to party with.

"I need to move back and take care of her. Her health is real bad now. She is going downhill fast," Tilly said as she cleaned the counter.

"What happened to the lady that was living with her? Wasn't she there to help after you moved out the last time?" Diane asked.

"She has family that need her in South Carolina. She is moving soon, and Mom can't be left alone anymore," Tilly answered.

"What about Bobby or Sis, you have your hands full." Diane still felt like a big sister to Tilly and wanted to solve her problems.

"Sis is still in Florida having babies every year. I don't know how they make it. Bobby is strung out all the time, and his wife left him.

He can't be counted on at all. I'm the only one left, it is me or nobody," Tilly said.

"That is how it has always been," Diane said, and got the broom to sweep.

"When I'm out of nursing school, my salary will make a difference. They are practically begging for nurses," Tilly said with a positive attitude. Diane put the broom down to wait on the couple who walked in the door. She was thinking about Tilly and school. She knew Tilly had been in school a couple of years on and off. She wondered if she would finally make it.

Tilly arrived at her home in her new-used Mini-Van. She was sitting looking around at her old home, it looked abandoned and lifeless. Hank and Matt were in the back pushing each other.

"Ya'll stop! Your Grandma will not feel like your shenanigans today," Tilly said, and took off her sunglasses. It was early fall and it was still pretty warm outside. She looked through the rearview mirror. Rae was in the very back seat with earphones on listening to her music. The boys jumped out finally and Tilly took a deep sigh. It was a cycle that she couldn't break, back at this home again and again.

"Oh, Tilly, I'm so glad you made it." It was Miss June coming down from the porch. "She is in a bad way," Miss June said softly after she gingerly went over the middle step and met Tilly. She looked around and greeted the kids.

"Sonny's not helping you move today is he?" Miss June asked hoping the answer would be "no" because she did not think Bonnie could take him today. Tilly told her that Sonny wasn't around, and hugged Miss June.

"It's a shame that Mrs. Berry couldn't stay with your mom. Bonnie took it bad when she left," Miss June said as they walked up to the porch.

"That's all right, we'll make the best of it," Tilly said and opened the door.

"I'm glad to have you near again. The Lord will bless you for taking care of your mom. Where are all your things?" Miss June asked looking back at the Van.

"I sold most of the big stuff and what didn't sell, I threw out the back," Tilly said laughingly. Miss June got the joke because she knew Tilly had lived next to a dump.

"I have a few more trips to make today and tomorrow," Tilly said.

When things had settled down, Miss June and Tilly were out on the porch drinking some coffee. Rae was in her room, and the boys were playing video games. Tilly was looking at the steps.

"That board I put down to replace that step last time I was here, didn't work too well," Tilly said breaking the silence.

"It needed to be the right size, now all the steps could use some work," Miss June observed.

"I'll try to get to that soon. The fig tree has really gotten big." Tilly looked over at the giant fig tree next to the porch.

"Yeah, it needs to be cut back. February is the time to do that." Miss June gave her wisdom out freely.

"The boys will have to go to the high school here in a couple of years. You know, this county still doesn't have middle schools. Have you signed them up for the school year?" Miss June finally said after a while.

"Yes, I've taken care of it. They will be there bright and early Monday morning. I don't know if I like the idea of them in high school in a couple of years, but it can't be helped," Tilly said.

"Rae is doing better, they will be all right. The schools are actually smaller here now. That may be a good thing for them. They build those new big schools now and I'm not so sure that is good for kids, I think they need to have fewer students in one place," Miss June was saying, and Tilly thought she should know, since she taught school for years. Tilly appreciated Miss June's advice on the schools.

"Have you heard from Tim Reynolds lately?" Miss June broke the silence to ask Tilly this question knowing that they had written to each other.

"Yes, he is in Africa for a while. He writes wonderful letters. Some of them are form letters sent to everyone he knows, but I've had a few personal letters," Tilly said shyly.

"Oh, my...well...well," Miss June teased.

"It was a dream to meet him, and to think I had such a crush on him growing up. He is just normal though and easy to communicate with. It's ironic that he had a role in the change in my life. Who would have thought," Tilly said contemplating things.

"I remember you having a fascination with Africa when you were young. You loved the mission stories at Vacation Bible School. It is nice you are able to write and keep up with Tim's adventures," Miss June said. Tilly's mind went back to those many summers at church. She could almost feel herself back in the small wooden chair listening to all the Bible and missionary stories. They both went back to that in their minds until the silence was broken by Bonnie's voice calling for some water. They both went in to attend to their patient.

Bonnie passed away a few months after Tilly had moved in. Sis came with all her kids and Bobby managed to stay sober enough to get through the funeral. They both made quick exits out of Tilly's life as soon as things were settled with the small estate. Bonnie had some money set aside, and Tilly had given the money to Sis and Bobby. Tilly was going to stay in the house. They did not care about the house anyway. Bobby got the car and Sis a lot of the furniture. Tilly had other things to settle legally and she took care of all that and started to live a normal life again.

Red had come to town for the funeral. He had offered to take the boys back with him for a while. She let him visit the boys everyday, but she would not let him have them for any length of time. She was afraid of Red's temper when he drank, and he drank often. Red was mad with Tilly. He drove up the last morning he was in town. He was mad and drunk. Tilly heard the truck out in the driveway and Red yelling.

"Tilly, I came to get the boys! You're not gonna stop me!" Red yelled at Tilly as she walked out on the front porch.

"Red you have the court order that you can visit. I complied with that. You know you can't take them." Tilly was referring to the last round of arguments in court over the children.

"The court order says I can have them for visits!" Red yelled.

"You can not have them now. You're drunk. Go home! You just want to cause trouble for me! Come back when you are sober!" Tilly yelled and started into the house.

"I want the boys...you selfish witch!" Red yelled as he stumbled out of the red pick-up and staggered toward Tilly.

"Red, I'm calling the police!" Tilly yelled opening the screen to go in when Red lunged up on the porch and grabbed Tilly's arm.

"You...you can't treat me this way...I'll teach ya a thing or two!" Red kicked her stomach hard and she fell in pain. He continued to kick her with his heavy boots.

"Red, stop it!" Tilly pleaded. Red took her by the hair and pulled her up hard. He shoved her toward the house.

"Go get the boys now!" Red ordered, and when Tilly looked back in defiance, Red punched her in the face. Blood was everywhere. Tilly pushed Red back and he stumbled on the steps backwards and fell down.

"Oh, you are getting rough now...well you've got it coming now!" Red went toward his truck. Tilly thought he might be leaving. Red, instead, reached in the truck and grabbed his riffle from the gun rack on the rear window. He walked toward Tilly. She froze. He could kill her and she knew it. The screen creaked open behind her. Hank Jr. walked out.

"Dad don't!" Hank yelled and ran out to his dad. Red swatted him aside. Matt came out crying and clung to his mom. Red continued to wave the gun at Tilly and yell obscenities.

"Get out of here Red!" It was Rae coming out of the door with a shotgun in her hands, and she knew how to use it. She had hunted with her dad on occasions. She now pointed the gun at Red.

"No!" Matt yelled, pushing Rae down, and the gun went off. Hank Jr. fell to the ground in a pool of blood. Everything seemed like it went in slow-motion for Tilly. She ran to Hank. She felt he was miles away and it took her forever to get there. She was yelling and praying. Rae and Matt were stunned still. Red dropped to the ground as if he was a dropped rag-doll. "No! What have I done?" He was tearing at himself. Tilly reached Hank and held him, crying and pleading to God to save her baby.

"Is he dead?" Red had crawled over to them.

"No, it's an arm wound, but it is bad. We have to stop the bleeding - give me your belt!" Tilly barked out orders. Suddenly her nursing education was kicking in full force.

"Mom...I'm so...so...sorry," Rae cried as she dropped to her knees beside her mom. When she saw the blood, she crawled under the fig tree and threw-up. Tilly could not help Rae right now, she had to focus on Hank Jr.

"Matt, call for help!" Tilly yelled to Matt, who was still standing on the porch. He quickly went toward the door but stopped when he heard Miss June. She was coming out of her yard toward them with towels in her hand. "I already called, they are on the way!" Miss June knelt beside Tilly to help her and Tilly gave her a thankful look.

"He'll be all right," Miss June said softly and they heard the sirens.

Hank Jr. suffered a bad upper arm wound. If it had not been for Tilly's quick thinking and nursing, he probably would have bled to death. He had months of physical therapy and a scar remained. Red was arrested for threatening his family and violating court orders. Rae was not charged with anything, it was considered as self-defense. She could have actually saved her mother's life in a round-about way. If things had not unfolded the way they did, Red could have killed Tilly.

Preacher James visited Tilly and the family after the incident; they had become regular church goers. Tilly was learning a lot about God, and Miss June was there helping them. Tim Reynolds had made a phone call to Tilly as soon as he heard about what had happened. Tilly was thankful for life at this point.

Chapter 16

1998-1999

A few years after Tilly made her peace with God, she graduated from nursing school with her family and friends looking on with proud faces. It was a great moment for Tilly. Tilly was still walking on clouds when she reached home after the small ceremony. There was a package waiting on the front porch. She opened it with Miss June looking on. The kids had run in to get food, uninterested in the package. It was a shoe box and inside was a pair of the best nursing shoes money could buy. Tilly looked at Miss June with thankfulness.

"They are not from me, read the card inside," Miss June said handing her the card. Tilly looked questioningly at Miss June and slowly opened the card. It read:

Tilly, get rid of those floppy waitress shoes and step into your new life in these. They are the best for the best girl I know. You'll make a great nurse.'

Love,
Tim

"He remembered those floppy shoes," Tilly laughed. She could not believe this. She read the card over and over again. Miss June went in to help the boys get something in the kitchen. Tilly finally went in and sat down at the kitchen table in a daze. She looked at Miss June.

"You knew about the shoes?" Tilly questioned Miss June.

"He called and wanted to know your size. I had to be sneaky about that. He wanted to know what day you would graduate and so on..." Miss June said as she shoved a sandwich toward Tilly. Tilly was too touched for words and ate her sandwich without really tasting it.

Tilly wrote a thank–you letter immediately. It went to Malawi, where Tim had been for some months. Letters were exchanged regularly. Tim described the small fishing village with detail. It was called Nkhata Bay. Tim wrote:

"We will be teaching the people of this area how to evangelize, and will be teaching them lessons from the Bible. The goal of the mission isn't to be the one who stays in an area constantly teaching and witnessing, the goal is to get the nationals to be able to work with the nationals."

The letter continued to describe the work there and the people. Tim was a good writer and Tilly was lost in his words. As Tim moved from area to area he wrote Tilly all the time. They became friends through the letters, and Tilly wrote her innermost thoughts to him. He also opened up to her. He started making a movie and directing it. He wanted it to "touch the world" as he put it in his letters. Tim was very busy and so was Tilly.

Tilly was working at the hospital nearby. Money was good and Tilly saved most of her money. She wanted college money for her children. Rae had been accepted at the University of Georgia. The boys were doing better at school. Things were calm for a while, and Tilly was happy with the letters from Tim. She knew he wrote to many people, but she felt they had become close.

The shoes Tim had given her had worn out with time and she had gotten new ones. She could not bring herself to get rid of those old shoes, and put them on as slippers to wear around the house. Time marched on so fast, as it often does.

Miss June became ill the year Rae went off to college. Tilly took care of Miss June until she became bed-ridden and she needed constant care. Nurses came and went, and no one in Miss June's family could stay long with her. Tilly decided to move Miss June in with her so she could take the best care of her. Tilly acquired a hospital bed and put it up in the front room. Rae helped on the weekends when she came home, and the boys helped at night when Tilly worked the night shift. When Tilly worked in the day, another nurse friend stayed with Miss June.

One warm May day, Tilly had the day off and Miss June was having a good day. They were enjoying a nice chat. There was a nice breeze coming in from the open door and the screen kept the buzzing insects outside. Tilly didn't want to put the air conditioner on yet and wanted to enjoy the fresh air. Besides, Miss June got cold so easily. There was the smell of a roast in the oven. Tilly was making a rare attempt for a big meal because Rae was coming home from college for a long weekend and the boys would come in starving like they always did. Miss June had a very good day and Tilly had the time to spend in the kitchen. Tilly was sitting in a chair beside the bed.

"You have done so much for me," Miss June spoke in a soft voice.

"Not nearly as much as you have done for me," Tilly said and took Miss June's hand.

Tilly got up and hugged Miss June, then turned away to wipe a tear from her cheek. She was startled by a figure at the door. She couldn't make out who it was because the sun was shinning in so brightly.

"Rae, is that you?" Tilly went toward the screen and a smile came across her face.

"Tim! Come in!" Tilly exclaimed.

Tim stepped in with two bunches of flowers. He hugged Tilly.

"I heard about Miss June. How is she?" Tim asked in a low voice. Miss June appeared to be sleeping

"It's her heart...I don't think she has much time," Tilly whispered. "This is breaking my heart. It is so good to see you, come on in."

"Has Rae come home? It is time for her," Miss June asked.

"No, Miss June. Guess who is here?" Tilly guided Tim over to the bed.

"Oh, it is Tim. This is a surprise," Miss June said and reached out for a hug. Tilly went to get two vases for the flowers. Tim put a sorted arrangement of flowers in one and put it beside the bed. He turned around with the roses.

"These are for you," He said and handed them to Tilly.

"Thank you. I will put these in front of the window. Aren't the flowers beautiful Miss June?" Tilly said.

"Oh yes and I can smell them," Miss June said weakly. Tilly moved them closer to Miss June and was unaware of Tim's eyes on her. When Miss June was asleep, Tim and Tilly walked out on the front porch.

"It is an incredible thing you are doing here for Miss June," Tim said as they sat down on the front porch swing with iced tea.

"It is the right thing to do. I wouldn't have it any other way. She did so much for me when I was growing up. She took care of us all the time. There was no one in her family who could take care of her. Her brothers and sisters all have passed away. Only one sister had children, and they don't live here. They talked to me about arranging a nursing home to put her in, but I have the training to take care of her. She was able to be in her own home with nursing until a few weeks ago. She doesn't have long now...and I needed to be with her," Tilly said, and cried. Tim reached over and hugged her.

"I'm so proud of you. You've come a long way. Where are the kids?" Tim asked.

"Rae will be coming in any minute for a long weekend. She has today and Monday off. And since it is Friday, the boys will come in happy

162

from school in a few minutes," Tilly said looking toward the road and wiping her tears. Tilly looked at her watch.

"I worry about Rae on the road when she comes home. The traffic is so bad, especially on Friday. I usually call her cell phone about three times before she gets home. She gets upset with me about my worrying," Tilly continued. Tim was looking at Tilly with a lot of love, and hugged her again.

"Rae's a smart girl, she'll be careful. She takes after her mom," Tim said.

"I was never that smart. She wants to be a doctor and she has the grades to do it. I was never that smart in school," Tilly said.

"Oh, I think, given different circumstances, you would have been just as good in school. You had a lot harder time," Tim said and lifted Tilly's chin and kissed her forehead.

"I was pretty wild. I've been blessed that Rae has straightened out and didn't follow in my footsteps," Tilly said and blushed a little. They caught each others eyes and there was a moment...and then the humming of the school bus could be heard.

"The boys are coming," Tilly said quickly as the bus stopped. The door flung open and the boys jumped out. Some one yelled out the window.

"Look its Tim Reynolds!" With that there was an eruption on the bus with kids hanging out yelling at Tim. Tim waved and laughed. The twins were instantly popular and they greeted Tim happily. They ran toward the house and Tilly shushed them. She told them Miss June was resting, and they quieted down as they entered the house. Tilly turned around to the road still watching for Rae. Tim got out his cell phone and said, "Call her." Tilly called and Rae was five minutes away. Tilly gave the phone back to Tim.

"I think I bug her too much," she said.

"Oh, you can't bug your children too much. My kids are grown and married and I still worry over them. When they lost their mom, I didn't know how to help them because I was so hurt. I worried about them. Hollywood was a hard place to grow up, especially in the movie business. They are strong now and I talk to them often," Tim said. A car horn blew and it was Rae in her red Toyota. Tilly let out a sigh of relief. This did not escape Tim's attention. Rae jumped out of the car and ran to greet them. She hugged her mom and Tim. They talked a minute and went toward the house. Rae stopped at the steps.

"I see you attempted to fix that middle step with yet another new board. These steps need a whole redo because they are uneven," Rae said and laughed.

"I know, I'm really going to brick them one day," Tilly said.

"She has been saying that for years," Rae said to Tim.

"I think I hear Miss June. I'll go check, excuse me," Tilly said as she walked into the house through the squeaky screen door. Rae turned to Tim and hugged him again.

"Thanks for coming. Mom looks so happy. Thanks too for all the exciting letters from Africa," Rae said. She had wanted to thank him so many times for what he brought to their lives.

"Don't thank me, I love to write to your mom and all you kids. Let me help you go ahead and get things out of the car while we are out here. I smell something good coming from the kitchen," Tim said as they walked back toward the car. Rae had only some laundry and a couple of bags. Rae had not missed the looks Tim was giving her mother. She knew that look. Tim was falling for her mom. When they both got in with the things, they followed the great smell to the kitchen. Tilly was checking on her roast and it was almost ready. She had cooked biscuits and fresh green beans that had come from her small garden out back.

"I hope you will stay and eat Tim," Tilly said.

"Oh, I'd love to," Tim said, rubbing his hands together as if he couldn't wait.

"Miss June is asleep," Rae said when she came back from the back room where she had deposited her things.

"She sleeps most of the time now," Tilly said as she got out the roast. Tim jumped to give her a hand. Rae was observing the whole thing.

"Well, I'll go in and wash my hands...excuse me," Tim said and went toward the hallway. Tilly was busily getting things out of the cabinet when Rae said, "He loves you." Tilly shut the cabinet and turned around. "What?" Tilly asked not believing her ears.

"You heard me," Rae said shyly.

"You are seeing more into this than there is. That is a nice thought, but Tim has lots of friends and some of them are probably women. They are way out of my league," Tilly said as she put the butter on the table. Tilly tapped her daughters arm as Tim entered the room. He felt he had interrupted something.

When they had eaten, they all decided to eat dessert later. They complimented Tilly on the dinner and scattered. Rae went to her room and the boys went to the recently enclosed screened porch. Tilly had it done for them to hang out in and play their games. They were so loud with the video games that this had been a good compromise.

Tilly did not like to clean the kitchen when she had company, preferring to spend that time visiting. It was always her way. This evening was no exception. She guided Tim out of the kitchen protesting. He wanted to help clean.

"There is always time to clean, but there is never enough time to spend with friends," Tilly said as they went to the front porch. They walked around the yard and smelled the roses that Tilly had started growing. She also had a small vegetable garden started. The smell of the magnolia tree next door filled the air. Tilly took in the smell with happiness as they reached the big fig tree at the edge of the yard.

"This is the biggest fig tree I've ever seen," exclaimed Tim.

"Yeah, it got away from me," Tilly replied.

"Do you eat the figs off of it? Tim asked.

"Yes, I have to fight the birds for them though. I make preserves sometimes. Miss June taught me how to do them. It will be a few weeks before we see any," Tilly said. Tim was watching Tilly and thinking how attractive she was.

"Because I saw thee under the fig tree, believest thou? Thou shalt see greater things than these..." Tim said.

"What?" Tilly was shook out of her thoughts.

"Oh, uh, it was a Bible verse that came to me, John 1:50. The tree reminded me of it. There are many verses in the Bible with a fig tree in them," Tim said. He noticed the evening sun going down. The dimming light seemed to be focused on Tilly.

"What does it mean?" Tilly asked.

"It's when Jesus saw Nathaniel under the fig tree. He was calling his disciples at the time," Tim explained.

"I'll have to read about that," Tilly replied.

Tim left to go to a hotel for the night. He was going to see Preacher James the next day. He told Tilly he would be back before he left.

When Tim was alone that night, he had time to reflect on things. He had done something that he thought he would not do again. He had fallen in love. How would he deal with this? He could not ask Tilly to live the kind of life he lived. She had children who needed her and a settled life, besides having to care for her "second mom." He couldn't tie her to a commitment that would tear her family apart. He prayed and decided to wait. He would write to her and see how things unfolded. He had commitments right now for a whole year. What if someone snatched her up? She certainly had the opportunities, according to Preacher James. Preacher James mentioned that a lot of single men at the church asked her out, but she seemed uninterested in any of them.

"That might not last..." he said to himself as he dozed on to sleep.

Tilly and Tim saw each other while Tim was in town. She was afraid of losing her heart and getting hurt, so she kept a wall up. Tim did not understand why Tilly kept her distance. He left on his plane without letting Tilly know his true feelings.

Miss June died right after the fourth of July. Tilly took this harder than anything she had ever been through. She grieved heavily. It was hard on the kids too. She was like a grandmother to them. Red's parents did not see the boys much and Sonny's parents had died years ago, so they had no grandparents that they could be close to. Miss June had offered them love and stability.

Tilly wrote to Tim. He was in Nigeria. He wrote such a kind and comforting letter back. It was full of encouragement for Tilly. Every time Tim wrote to her, she looked for deeper meanings. She hoped secretly for more. She had lost herself in love and had frequently been distracted. Tilly read that he was coming back to the states in a few months. Tilly did not read why he was coming back; just that he was coming back. That was a comfort to her and got her through the difficult time ahead.

Tilly and the boys went to church almost every Sunday now. Rae went too, when she wasn't staying at the college on weekends. She did not come home as often as she used to. She had a boyfriend and that kept her away from home more. Rae had brought him home once and he seemed nice, but Tilly reserved her thoughts on the situation until a later day. Tilly wanted Rae to finish her school and not get serious.

The boys were in the freshman year of high school. They had managed to find friends of the worst kind. They started the year off wrong and skipped school often. Tilly thought they had seen the truth last year and were doing better, but this year, she did not know what to think of their behavior. She went to Preacher James and he offered advice.

"I'm sure they must be into drugs or something or they wouldn't act this way," Tilly explained to Preacher James.

"Get them involved in church and a job. I'll talk to them too," Preacher James said.

Tilly talked to Rae about the situation one rare weekend when they were together.

"Mom, don't nag, that will not help. They are going to have to come to their own conclusion that there is no point to their behavior. I'll spend more time here and with them for a while," Rae said as she grabbed a soda out of the refrigerator and sat down on the sofa. Tilly rubbed the side of her head. Rae observed her mom.

"You have another one of your headaches?" Rae asked.

"Yes, I took something for it a few minutes ago. I'll be better soon," Tilly replied.

"What scares me is that their dad never got better. He has lived his life in and out of jail. He has been married to two more wives since me and now he is in for life for killing someone. I see the same temper in the boys, and even more in Hank Jr.," Tilly said wearily after a moment of silence between the two.

"Mom, Sonny never straightened out much either, but look at me, I'm all right," Rae said and took her moms hand. "It will be all right with the boys too, they know better and they are just testing the waters. They'll come around," Rae said, and finished the soda. She went to the kitchen and came back.

"Have you heard from Sonny and Diane recently? I can't believe those two are still together. They are such a mess. They must keep each other going, I guess." Rae had grabbed a banana on her way back to the front room. She proceeded to open it and eat it.

"You are probably right, they keep each other going. Sonny did call yesterday to see if you were coming home this weekend. I told him you would call him," Tilly said.

"I'll call him," Rae said as she bit into the banana. "Where is Tim these days?"

"Oh, he is in Nigeria. I worry about his safety since missionaries are a target in certain areas of Africa," Tilly said.

"When is he coming to see you," Rae asked slyly. Tilly smiled.

"He said this Christmas, maybe," Tilly answered. "I can't believe it's almost another year coming up, time flies.

"Well, Mom, you can't spend your entire life dreaming about Tim. I want something to happen between you... but maybe you should go out...with some other men... maybe from church. What about Mr. Brown, he is nice and good-looking," Rae continued.

"What has gotten into you? I'm not interested in anyone else. I know...Tim may not ever be ready to settle into a serious relationship, but the dream is all I need...I mean he has been in my dreams since I was twelve. I like it this way...I mean, how many people get to have a dream come true. Besides he does talk about...loving me...and how difficult it would be for us if we were married." Tilly was talking and the look of a stunned Rae stared back at her.

"Mom, he is serious! Why didn't you tell me?" Rae asked.

"Because, it is so complicated. He is committed to his mission work... and that is good. The mission work doesn't include me right now," Tilly said, and Rae sat still deep in thought.

Chapter 17

Fall 1999

Tilly sat in church one Sunday evening taking in the surroundings. She had chosen to sit in the back instead of up-front with the rest of the single group. She wasn't into that group. The small talk was boring. She was restless and confused, and she needed time to pray alone. Dan Brown always wanted to sit with her and sometimes put his arm on the back of the pew behind her as if to say "She's mine." Tilly thought he was nice and good-looking. He was the cream of the crop here. He wasn't the first guy to ask her out in the four years of attending church on a regular basis, and he probably wouldn't be the last. She had tried to date a few of them with an open mind, but just couldn't get into it. Tilly had eventually pulled away from the single group and went to help the pre-school division. That gave her satisfaction and a feeling of being needed. In the summers Tilly went to work in a place close to her heart - Vacation Bible School. She moved her work schedule and took vacation time to work with the children. She loved that time. Her kids

174

loved it too, until they were too old to go. They continued to help in the program when they got older, and that kept the boys out of trouble, at least for a week. Rae helped her every day, but the boys would help on their terms. They came late and missed a day or two. Tilly figured a little help from them was better than none and she let them be. She sat here in the back of the church still thinking about all this. The music started at the end of the sermon and she was startled out of her thoughts. The invitation to go up front and pray was indicated and Tilly sat still. Her heart was heavy for her boys. She put her head down and wept. She was tired, tired of climbing that uphill battle with life. She knew she had a lot to be thankful for, and she thanked God for her blessings. Rae also worried her now that she had this new boyfriend. Tilly wasn't too sure of him. Rae had stayed at school yet another weekend. Tilly was lonely and found herself trying to find words in Tim's letters that would give her hope. She was tired of that exercise too. She needed to change things. When the music finished, Tilly quickly made her way to the back door. She had almost made it to the car. She heard someone calling, but kept going.

"Hey...hey Tilly, wait up!" It was Dan Brown. Tilly rolled her eyes, thinking she had almost made it. She felt his hand on her shoulder and turned around and gave her best smile. She needed to be nice, nothing was his fault.

"Hey what's up? You don't sit with us anymore. Are you a snob now?" Dan asked laughing.

"No...I just had to be alone a little while. It's nothing personal," Tilly replied.

"Good, I'm glad it is not me...or maybe it is me and I stink." He pretended to smell under his arm. They both laughed. Tilly shook with the chill in the air. She had only worn a sweater. It had been a beautiful warm October day, but now it was cooling off and the day had given way to darkness.

"Are you going to the Fall Festival this weekend?" Dan asked.

"Yes, I always love to go to the Festival. I like the handmade crafts, but I'm afraid I buy too much," Tilly said still shivering.

"You deserve to buy what you want. Look at you, you are cold. Do you want to go for some coffee or something?" Dan asked.

"Uh..." Tilly stammered and looked around at the group staring at them from the front of the church. Some people had never let Tilly forget her past, and she felt their stares. She felt they saw her as below them. She had let no one know that Tim still wrote to her. It was her secret and they didn't deserve to know.

"Oh, don't worry. We can go somewhere else besides Billy's," Dan said quickly when he realized the situation. "There is a new coffee shop in mid-town and they would never go there." He glanced at the group. He knew they were talking about Tilly and wondering about him. He didn't care what they thought. Tilly saw the determined look on Dan's face. He was nice-looking and rich. He could have any one of those single ladies, but he had asked her out. She made up her mind.

"Yes... let's go to the new coffee shop. I'll have to check on the boys first though. I'll go use the church phone," Tilly said decidedly.

"Oh, you can use my cell phone," Dan said, and Tilly made the call. They had a pleasant time. Tilly realized what she had been missing, someone to talk to, not just write to. She decided to go out more.

Tilly went out with Dan some on and off. She wrote Tim with the thought in mind that she had to get on with her life. Tim seemed serious about her in his letters, but she was skeptical. She never let anyone know about Tim's letters except the children.

One evening after a date with Dan, they pulled into the driveway of the house. There were cars everywhere, and noises coming from the house. Dan went around to let a puzzled Tilly out of the car.

"What's going on? Is there a party?" Dan asked.

"I hope not," Tilly answered impatiently. She got out and walked to the porch, turning to warn Dan of the unstable front steps. They climbed the steps and opened the screen of the noisy house. Teenagers were everywhere, drunk or high on something. Matt and Hank saw their mom and quickly knew to get everyone out. They scrambled around practically pushing people out and yelling. The place was a mess. Tilly stood looking at her boys. She could tell they would not be capable of answering any of her questions, and she was so mad she couldn't talk to them. A scream came from the back and a young teenage girl ran out of the back bedroom chased by Mike, one of Hank's friends. They were laughing and screaming as they ran. They pushed past Tilly and through the screen, stumbling down the steps and laughing even harder when they landed on the ground. Tilly rolled her eyes.

"Wasn't that Deacon Ed's son, Mike?" Dan asked.

"Yes, but they'll deny he was even at my house." Tilly knew it would be fruitless to confront the parents.

"Well...uh...I guess I need to go. Will you be all right?" Dan asked.

"Yes, thank you." Tilly walked Dan to the car.

"Sorry," Tilly said simply.

"It's okay. I'll call you," Dan said. Tilly waved at him as he drove off. Tilly stood crying, knowing she would not hear from Dan again. Dan had one son who had done everything right, and a wife who had been perfect before she died. He did not understand and probably wouldn't want to. She knew instinctively that he would not be back around.

Tilly wrote to Tim and spilled out her heart. She even wrote about Dan and the reaction he had. She was right, he only spoke to her at church from that day on. Tim wrote back with news that he was coming home for Christmas. He would be going to see his children, and wanted to see Tilly to discuss something with her. Tilly had no idea about what Tim would want to talk to her about that he couldn't write in a letter, like always. She was almost afraid of what he wanted to tell her.

Chapter 18

1999-2000

Tilly taught pre-school Sunday School and got busy with many things at church. That was her way when she was down. She got busy and helped others. She enjoyed teaching the little ones each Sunday.

One Sunday, she was working closely with the children when Amanda pulled on her sleeve.

"I gotta go," Amanda said, dancing around as if to have to go the bathroom. Tilly looked over to her teen-age assistant.

"Leigh Ann, Amanda needs to go to the bathroom again. I'll take her this time." Tilly took Amanda's hand and went down the hall to the bathroom. Amanda skipped in and Tilly leaned heavily on the wall to wait.

"Hey, did you hear? Tim Reynolds is coming to town for Christmas. I can't wait!" It was Susan Miller speaking from around the corner. They could not see Tilly.

"And you can't wait to get your claws on him," Sara Bennett said and laughed.

"Stop it! Well I did go with him for coffee once, and I do get his letters. I write back, and you never know," Susan shot back. Tilly recognized Brenda Baker's and Amy Hall's voices. They were outside their singles group room. Tilly stood still, she couldn't believe her ears. She wasn't special after all.

"You know that Tilly will try to see Tim. He has shown interest in her," Amy said.

"Oh give me a break. He thinks of her like any missionary would, you know, a lost woman in need of guidance," Susan said, the voices fading as they went down the hall to their room. Tilly stood frozen to the wall. Tears steamed down her face. Amanda was pulling on her.

"Miss Tilly, can we go back now?" Tilly shook herself out of the shock and wiped her eyes quickly. She led Amanda back to the room and put up a good front.

When Tilly got into the car to drive home, she let herself go again. There was no one around and she cried. She had blown it with Dan, and now she found out that she never had a chance with Tim. She was cried out before she reached home to fix lunch for Rae and the boys. She had gotten good at covering up her feelings. Rae noticed something, but didn't ask her, and the boys wouldn't notice if she turned her hair purple.

Tilly threw herself into work at the hospital, even taking extra hours. If she wasn't working, she was trying to track the twins down. They stayed out late sometimes, but they were showing signs of improvement. She was thankful for any little improvement in her life. They had gotten back into some youth activities at church, thanks to Preacher James.

"Mom, Dad and Diane asked me over for Thanksgiving," Rae declared. She was on school break for the Thanksgiving holiday. She looked at Tilly with sympathy. She did not want to leave her mom.

"Well, maybe you should go. They never ask you over much," Tilly replied.

"That is the point. I don't know why they asked me," Rae said as she folded her newly washed and dried clothes. She frequently brought her hamper of dirty clothes to wash when she came home. They had settled in the front room. Tilly was drinking some coffee. It was a bit chilly outside, but otherwise it was a beautiful sunny day.

"Maybe you shouldn't ask why. You should just go. They seem to be reaching out," Tilly said.

"I don't want to leave you on Thanksgiving." Rae sat next to her mom on the couch and took her hand.

"I will have the twins here. They at least eat with me," Tilly said laughing.

"They've laid low since their encounter with the police the other night," Rae said referring to the police catching them speeding. There had been some vandalism in the area and they were hauled off to the jail for questioning. The police eventually found a gang that was picked up a few hours later with evidence that they were the guilty ones. The boys were let go with a speeding ticket that they were still trying to take care of. Hank might lose his license over it. Tilly thought it would teach him a lesson if he did lose his driving privilege. They had just got their licenses as it was.

"You haven't said anything about Tim lately," Rae said as she got up to continue to fold clothes.

"Well...you know I still get his letters. Sometimes I write back. He writes a lot of people and a lot of people write him. He is coming around here for Christmas. I may even see him," Tilly said and took a sip of her coffee. Rae looked at her. There was something else going on besides the loss of Mr. Brown. The boys had told her about that evening. Her mom seemed sad these days, but Rae did not push her about it.

Thanksgiving morning came and Rae was up early in the kitchen making coffee. Tilly stood a moment at the door watching her mature daughter puttering in the kitchen. She was so proud of her. Rae turned around to see her mom at the door.

"Good morning," Rae greeted Tilly.

"You are awful cheerful this morning. It must have something to do with that phone call you got late last night," Tilly said probing for information.

"You heard the phone? I'm sorry. It was Trent Goss. He is a friend. He is already in med. school. We have a lot in common," Rae said dreamily.

"Oh no..." Tilly started to say more and decided to take the peace offering of coffee and sit down.

"Mom...I know what you are thinking. Don't. We are dating...some. I am determined to get to med. school too. Nothing will mess that up," Rae said, determined.

"I know you are determined now, but we all know what love can do to the decisions made in the future. Believe me!" Tilly exclaimed.

"Mom, I know...I did not come this far for nothing," Rae said assuring her mom.

"You are much smarter than me... that is for sure," Tilly said as she got up to hug her daughter.

"If it wasn't for you, I wouldn't be where I am today," Rae said as they hugged.

"What time are you going to your dad's?" Tilly asked as she sat back down wiping a tear away. This was not lost on Rae.

"Mom, I can still back out. I can go later tonight to visit them, like I used to," Rae quickly said, misunderstanding the meaning of the tears from Tilly.

"Oh no...you should go. I hear they are finally tying the knot during the Christmas Holidays," Tilly said.

"Yeah they are making it official after all these years. Can you believe it? Well they always said they were married, so they might as well have it on paper," Rae replied back.

At noon that Thanksgiving Day, Rae left for her dad's home. Sonny had bought a piece of land outside of Atlanta and had built the house that he had always wanted. His body shop had done well through the years as he mellowed out. Diane, to everyone's surprise, had been behind Sonny's success even though they both still liked to party.

Tilly stood at the new screen door she had recently bought. She waved to Rae until she was out of sight. Rae blew her horn as she rounded the curve up the way. It was a warm day for Thanksgiving so Tilly left the main door open and went to check on the boys.

They were still asleep. She went back to the kitchen to check on the turkey. She heard a knock at the door. It had to be Rae back, she probably forgot something, Tilly thought. She must have latched the screen or Rae would have come on in.

"Did you forget something?" Tilly yelled from the kitchen, wiping her hands on the towel. There wasn't an answer as she walked out of the kitchen. She looked out of the screen door and gasped, dropping the towel on the floor.

"Hey! Well, are you going to let me in?" It was Tim. Tilly resisted opening the door and throwing herself in his arms. The words from the hallway at church came back to her as she unlatched the door. Tim swung open the door and picked Tilly up off her feet. He did something totally unexpected. He kissed her long and hard. Tilly was in shock.

"Well aren't you gonna say something? Aren't you glad to see me? Wow, it smells good in here." Tim was talking so fast Tilly could not respond. He looked around a moment and turned to Tilly.

"I...uh...what are you doing here? I mean...I thought you were coming later...like at Christmas. I am so glad to see you though," Tilly responded.

"I know I told you that, but I decided to come back sooner. It's a long story, I'll tell you later," Tim said cocking his head at Tilly as if to question her response to him.

"You just surprised me, that's all," Tilly said quickly. Tim turned toward the kitchen when they both heard a sizzling noise.

"Oh, that is my potatoes boiling!" Tilly exclaimed as she picked up the towel off the floor and scampered to take care of the potatoes. Tim followed her.

"I hope you can stay and eat. I understand if you have other plans though." Tilly talked over her shoulder as she worked. Tim stood at the doorway with his arms crossed.

"I don't have any other plans. I was in California earlier this week for my granddaughter's birth. She was a bit premature. That is one of the reasons I'm back early," Tim explained as he opened the oven door to check the turkey. Tilly turned around from the sink.

"Is the baby all right?" Tilly asked.

"Oh yes, she is fine." Tim took in the smell of the turkey. "Gonna be a good one," Tim said referring to the turkey.

"I didn't know you were expecting a grandchild," Tilly said.

"I thought I wrote you about it," Tim replied.

"No, is your daughter all right?" Tilly asked as she got out the dishes.

"Here, let me help you. Yes, she is fine," Tim said as he grabbed the dishes out of Tilly's hand. She noticed he was smiling from ear to ear just like a proud granddad. She loved him even more at that moment, but she knew she couldn't have him.

"You know, I write so many letters, I forget who I write what to. I certainly did not leave that information out on purpose. I'm just getting old and forgetful," Tim said, misunderstanding the look that Tilly was giving him. When he mentioned all the letters he wrote, Tilly remembered the over-heard conversation in the hall at church again.

"I uh...guess you will see Susan Miller while you are here. Sit down and I'll go get the boys." Tilly scampered out of the kitchen leaving Tim puzzled. Tilly came back in and the boys bounded in hungry. They were glad to see Tim and almost knocked him down greeting him. A lot of talk flew across the table with tales of Tim's travels and the boys asking all kinds of questions. They were shoveling the food in as fast as they talked. The boys finally left when they had their fill. They had planned on seeing a new movie at the theater and had already bought the tickets. The house was quiet when they left and the kitchen was a wreck. Tilly decided to clear some of the dishes and leave most of it for later.

"When they get back, they'll have dessert," Tilly said laughing. Tim helped clean the table. He noticed something was the matter with Tilly. She wasn't her usual self. Small talk continued and was strained.

"Tilly, who is Susan Miller?" Tim finally had to ask.

"You know Susan. She said she went out with you when you were in town last time. You write to her all the time," Tilly said impatiently. Tim stopped and thought for a moment.

"Oh, I did stop at a coffee shop outside of town before I went to the airport last year...I think it was last year. Anyway there was a Susan somebody from the church who happened to come in. Yes...she was a very attractive lady... if I remember correctly. I remember...I put her on my list to write to her. She gets my newsletter just like everyone else. I think she has written, but I'm too busy to respond to every letter. I just communicate through my newsletters," Tim explained.

"You mean you don't write her personal letters?" Tilly asked.

"No. Well...I may have put a personal note in some of the earlier newsletters, but that was it. I do that sometimes," Tim answered.

"Oh. Would you like some pie or something with coffee?" Tilly asked quickly.

"Yes. We'll sit out on the front porch and talk. It is nice outside. It is kind of warm for Thanksgiving," Tim said sensing something wasn't right. They got the pie and coffee and settled on the front porch swing. There was a silence.

"Tilly, were you jealous of Susan? Did she say something to you?" Tim asked.

"Jealous?" Tilly asked as if she did not know what Tim was saying.

"You know you are my only girl," Tim said as he put his pie down on the small side table on the porch. He took Tilly's hand.

"Really?" Tilly asked.

"Yes you are," Tim said and reached in his jeans pocket, pulling out something like a small box.

"Surely you got some idea about how much I cared about you through my letters. Oh I know I'm not much for words, but I thought you knew. When you started dating some guy named...oh I don't remember...well anyway, I thought I had waited too long. When you wrote heart broken about the boys and about him...well... it hurt. I wanted to fly home right away. I didn't blame you for going on with your life because I knew I was no catch way in Africa. I'm back for a while and I hoped...well," Tim stammered for words.

"Those ladies at church...I thought. They think I'm your project...you know the fallen woman in need of direction. I didn't know what to think. They make me feel that they are better than me, and they don't miss a chance to make it clear," Tilly blurted out. Tim laughed.

"No wonder you have been acting funny. Those ladies at church need a life," Tim said as he caught Tilly looking at the small box.

"You know, I should put this back in my pocket and not show you what's in it. You and your lack of faith in us...No, I'll just put it back and we will forget it." Tim was joking and made as if he were putting the box away. Tilly laughed and grabbed the box. When she got it, she froze. She was afraid to open it.

"Well, if you don't open it, you won't know what's in it," Tim said. Tilly bit her lower lip and slowly opened the box. A beautiful diamond ring glimmered inside. She held her hand to her heart as if to slow it down, it was beating so fast. She swallowed hard and was shaking. This had to be a dream.

"I hope your answer is yes. I mean... if it's not, there is always Susan," Tim said teasing.

Tilly looked up at him with tears streaming down her face and laughed.

"Yes!" She said it louder than she meant to and threw her arms around Tim. She hugged him and they talked until they heard the sound of the twins' car pull in the driveway. They came up talking loudly about the great movie they had just seen. Tilly and Tim laughed and followed them in so they could get their dessert. This was real life, but for a moment, it had felt like a fairy-tale. Tilly was completely happy for the first time in her life.

Thanksgiving flew by with Tim in and out. That Saturday was another beautiful day, and Tim and Tilly took a walk. They found themselves under the big fig tree, shy of all its leaves now. They discussed the future. Tim's plan included a move to California, where his children were. Private school was discussed for the twins. Tilly bristled at this. The twins had another year-and-a- half left in school. They would finish their junior year and then move. That would be their senior year at a different school. That was bad enough, but to go to a private setting would be way different than they were used to.

"What is the matter with private school? That might be just what they need to stay out of trouble," Tim said.

"I...I don't know. The boys..." Tilly started to say.

"The boys need a good school. They need to think of college and they need the best possible place for that. It would be the best for them. The public schools there would only offer more trouble for them," Tim replied.

"No, it is not just about the schools. I know my boys. A private school won't keep them from trouble. It has to come within themselves to rise above temptation. They would find trouble anywhere right now. The public schools are good enough for the twins. That is all they are used to." Tilly pleaded with Tim who had an amazed look on his face.

"What? Why are you looking at me like that?" Tilly asked Tim.

"Well for one thing, people don't send their children to public school where we would be living. You are right too. The boys do have to face life and make the right choices. My two certainly made a lot of wrong choices too, but I tried to provide the best way for them that I could," Tim said.

"I understand what you are trying to do. For some kids private school would be great and maybe straighten them out. A couple of years ago I might have jumped at a chance for private school for the kids, but they will have one year left and that is hard enough. And besides...since when were you a snob?" Tilly asked impatiently.

"It is not that I am a snob, but I do know what would be the best. Look you are right, there are some good public schools around the area. It might be harder going to school with me as their step-father...I mean safety is an issue you know," Tim said and Tilly gasped.

"I had not thought of that," Tilly said.

"Well I could commute you know. West to East coast until they finish school here." Tim threw out a last effort idea.

"No...No. I think they need a change from the influence here. I haven't had time to think of the changes for us all. I mean, the people you know and the places you've been. We may not fit in with your circle," Tilly was saying.

"Hey...Hey... None of that! I don't have a circle that I fit into," Tim said hugging Tilly. Tilly shuddered from the coolness of the evening air.

"It's cooling off a bit. Let's build a fire in the fireplace and have some coffee," Tim continued as they walked toward the house. Tilly and Tim got the firewood from the corner of the house. Tilly had the fireplace cleaned just before fall at a good price. She had not built a fire in the fireplace for years. Tilly was glad that she had everything ready for a good fire. She learned that Tim liked cozy fires, but seldom got to have one in the climates he lived in. Georgia didn't get very cold for long periods of time, but at least they had a winter.

They fell into a silence after a while in front of the fire. The boys were gone for the evening and it was real quiet. The popping of the firewood was the only noise. Tim looked at Tilly.

"I hope you are not worried about everything, because it will work out... Everything will work out. You will see," Tim said reassuring Tilly. Tim told her that he was speaking the next day at the service. He wanted to announce their engagement, but Tilly was hesitant. It took some talking on Tim's part, but before he left he had convinced Tilly to go along with him to church and make the announcement. She had not even worn the ring around town yet. He kissed her at the car door and got in.

"Don't worry. It'll be fine. See ya bright and early, all right?" Tim said and cranked the car. Tilly nodded. She waved to him until he was out of sight.

Sunday morning came and Tilly had fixed breakfast for the boys. Tim came in the front door as Tilly was yelling down the hall for the boys to eat. Tilly turned around and walked right into Tim's open arms before she knew what had happened. He gave her a great big hug and they both laughed.

"You scared me," Tilly said still laughing. Tim still hung on to her. "Let go of me, I have to get the boys up and going," Tilly demanded teasingly and Tim let go.

"Sure does smell good," Tim said as he went toward the kitchen. Tilly came back with the boys trailing behind her, hair ruffled and half asleep.

"Do we have to go to church? I have a headache," Hank Jr. complained.

"Oh, I think you can make it," Tilly replied, dishing up some pancakes as Hank sat down. Matt slumped down next and looked at Tim.

"You are here early," he declared.

"Didn't you tell them?" Tim asked Tilly.

"Tell us what?" Hank asked as he took a bite out of his pancakes. Matt just stared at them.

"We are planning to make an important announcement at church this morning," Tim said as he finally sat down.

"No...well I don't think that is a good idea. We can tell...you know...but not make an announcement," Tilly stammered.

"What?" Matt asked. Hank put his fork down. He punched Matt with his elbow.

"Look at her hand," he said.

"Oh, I see," Matt said.

"Does Rae know?" Hank asked.

"Yes, I called her late last night," Tilly replied.

"Look, I don't care to go to church, especially today," Hank grumbled and went to his room. Matt silently finished his food and went after his brother.

"That went well," Tilly said sarcastically.

"Don't worry. Kids that age worry about their own lives changing. Things will change for them Tilly, but don't worry they'll come around. We had better hurry, I need to be out of here in fifteen minutes," Tim said as he started clearing the table.

"Wow, you clean up after yourself too. I'll go hurry the boys," Tilly said and went down the hall. Hank was back in bed with the cover up over his head. Tilly gently pulled the cover down.

"There is no getting out of it today. You are not going to make me go through this alone," Tilly said. Hank jumped past her and ran into the bathroom. She heard the shower turn on. Matt turned around from the closet he was rummaging through.

"Man, I can't find anything to wear. You know I have to take a shower too and Hank takes forever," he said. Tilly shook her head and went back to the front room where Tim was pacing.

"Tim, the boys always make me late on Sunday. You go. I know you want to talk to Preacher James before the services. We'll be along. I can't risk leaving with you or the boys won't come at all," Tilly said.

"Are you sure you are not ducking out on me?" Tim asked as he turned toward the door.

"Tim, I'm not sure about this announcement business." Tilly pleaded one more time.

"I am sure...and don't go sit in the back. You come right up front," Tim said as he walked gently down the front steps. Tilly waved at him until he was out of sight. She went in to hurry the boys.

The boys were still grooming themselves as they walked out to the van, still in no hurry. The van, now ten years old, was pretty sad looking. What once was a shiny red van had become, through the years, a drab, dented, beat up, old dirty vehicle.

"Mom, let us drive our car," Hank said, standing with his socks and shoes in his hands. Hank and Matt had gone in together and bought an old dark blue car. Tilly had not minded because it was a safe car, but they poured money into it to keep it going. Sonny had helped some by giving them all a break on repair prices. Right now the boys were taking a stand together not to ride with their mom to church. They would much rather drive their cool car and not be embarrassed by this poor excuse for a van. Tilly lost her patience.

"No! Why do you think I waited on you?" she yelled.

"Mom! Wow! Calm down! We will follow you...we promise!" Matt exclaimed. Tilly did not want to argue in the front yard and she knew they were determined.

"Okay, I'll be looking in my rear view mirror. No stopping at the burger joint drive-thru. Tilly opened the driver's side door with a determined look on her face. The boys complained, but that is exactly what they had planned on doing. They were bottomless pits, and eating was always on their minds. They were in no hurry as Tilly pulled out and waited. She wasn't going to let them out of her sight. They thought if they took a lot of time she would finally pull off. She knew better.

On the way Tilly frequently looked in the mirror to check on them. She could tell they had their radio blasting and they were cutting up. She had told them not to cut up in the car, but they did anyway. She shook her head.

She would have to have a talk with them. She heard them blast their car horn. They yelled at a jogger going past. No one was exempt from their torment. When they reached the two-lane road, the boys blasted around her, yelling. They were trying to make her pay for making them go to church. They knew she would be upset with the speed they were going.

"Just wait till I get my hands on you two!" Tilly yelled out the window. They did not hear her. It would serve them right to get caught by the police, Tilly thought. When Tilly arrived at the church parking lot, she saw them leaning on their car, grinning from ear to ear. She got out of the car.

"Where have you been Mom? Yeah, where ya been?" they both asked laughing. Tilly slammed the door and gave them the "look".

"Get inside! Now!" Tilly exclaimed and the boys quickly obeyed.

Tilly heard the organ music as they stepped into the church vestibule. It was the beginning of the service and people were making their final greetings while making their way to the seats. The boys slumped on the back seat and she motioned them to follow her. They shook their heads. She was on her own as she made it to the front pew. This was painful. She felt everyone was looking at her.

Her face grew hot as she slid down into her seat. She looked up to notice Susan plainly flirting with Tim. Susan hugged Tim, and Tim's eyes fell on Tilly over Susan's shoulder. He waved and walked up the steps to the pulpit area. Susan sat down practically on top of Tilly.

"Oh Tilly, I didn't know you were there. You don't normally sit here," Susan whispered. Tilly just shrugged. Susan leaned back over.

"I just asked Tim to lunch," Susan whispered, satisfied with herself.

"What did he say?" Tilly asked curiously.

"Oh, the music started and he didn't have a chance to answer. I'm sure he'll come," Susan said putting her hand on Tilly's arm. Tim was observing the two. Tim smiled at Tilly and Susan fluffed her hair and smiled at Tim, thinking Tim's smile was for her.

The music started and everyone stood to sing. Tilly looked back to check on the boys. She saw that Dana Coty was sitting by them. Hank Jr. fancied himself in love with this blond-haired beauty. Tilly wasn't sure of Dana's feelings. When she caught Hank's lovesick look, he motioned toward Dana with his head and smiled at his mom. Tilly smiled back. She could see a mischievous look on Matt's face. He was going to kid Hank about this. Tilly knew this would happen as soon as

Dana was out of sight. There was always a rivalry between the two, and Hank had been the first to notice the ravishing blond hair.

The music stopped and Preacher James got up to introduce his long-time friend, Tim Reynolds. The church was packed to hear Tim speak. Tim went to the podium and cleared his voice.

"It is so good to be back here with you today. This feels like a second home to me, and the warmth that I feel here makes me want to be here often. It is good to see Preacher James and all the good friends I have made here," Tim said and looked over at Tilly. "I write to many people here and I enjoy the letters from you all. I have become very close to one great lady here among you," Tim continued, and looked over again at Tilly. Susan smiled and looked at her friends. She gave Tilly a smirk.

"Well anyway, I would like her to come up here and stand beside me." He reached out his hand toward Tilly. Tilly and Susan started up, but Tilly gave Susan a look that made her slide back down in embarrassment. Tilly thought her heart would pound right out of her chest, and she couldn't feel her legs as she grabbed Tim's hand at the top of the steps. Tim felt her shaking.

"It's okay...we are in this together," he whispered in her ear. He kissed her cheek, and this was not missed among Susan and her cronies. They shook their heads at each other as if confused.

"I would like to make an announcement. This lovely lady has accepted my offer to become my wife," Tim said quickly, and waited because there was gasping and rumbling through the building. Susan and her friends sat motionless. After a moment there was some applause and shouting of approval. When it had calmed down, Tim continued to talk of the future plans that he and Tilly had discussed. They would be staying in the States for a while for Tim to make a movie that had been planned. They would travel to Africa after that.

Preacher James got up to do a short sermon, and a hymn was sung at the end, but Tilly felt as if it was all unreal. Susan never looked her way, and when they were dismissed, the group stalked away with a snide remark. "What did she do to get him?" they whispered. "Yeah, I wonder."

Tilly felt better as they were finally making their way to the parking lot. Tim was caught by someone on the way and motioned Tilly on. Tilly walked a short distance when someone grabbed her arm. She turned around and looked into the face of her brother. She had not seen him in years. He had been in and out of jail on minor charges, and had a substance abuse problem. He had a couple of children that he seldom saw.

"Bobby!" Tilly exclaimed as she hugged him.

"I heard the big announcement. I slipped in beside the boys in the back and I was just talking to them. I went by the house this morning and figured you were here. Well aren't you going to introduce me to your new fiancé?" Bobby asked as he observed Tilly's mouth open unable to speak. Tim had walked up.

"Oh...uh...yes. Tim, this is my brother Bobby, and Bobby, this is Tim Reynolds," Tilly managed to blurt out and they shook hands. Bobby knew Tilly was writing to Tim through an earlier phone call to Rae one time, but he was surprised by this turn of events. They exchanged some small talk and decided to pick up chicken for lunch. Bobby happily accepted the offer to join them. Tim went back to talk to Preacher James, with plans to come as soon as he could get away. When Tim left them Bobby turned to Tilly.

"Well, I had no idea you were this serious with Tim Reynolds. I thought it was just a nice long-distance friendship. Who knew?" Bobby said as he opened the car door for Tilly.

"Bobby...I'm just as surprised as you are... I mean I've loved him for a long time, but I dared not hope. I mean...well you know...he's dated a lot of women. I didn't think that of all those beautiful women, he would pick me," Tilly stammered.

"Oh, I'm not surprised he fell in love with you," Bobby replied quickly and hugged her through the open window. "See ya later," he said.

Tilly bought the chicken and drove home. She spotted Bobby's old truck in the driveway. She wondered that it still ran by the looks of it. When she got in, she immediately prepared some vegetables and had a nice talk with Bobby. He wondered if Sis knew, and Tilly said she had called her already. Tim arrived and they sat around the table chatting about the future. Bobby said he was wanting to settle back near home. Tilly looked at Tim.

"Well... Tilly won't be needing this home very much longer and she does not need to sell it. Perhaps she would like it if you could live here. Of course those steps need fixing and a few other things," Tim said and the boys laughed about the steps, but they soon got serious when they realized the changes they would have to go through. They started balking about a move.

"We have to discuss this you two. You have to be open to our plans," Tilly said to the boys as they argued again.

"Mom, I know things are going to change, but not this fast... I mean... you know," Hank Jr. blurted out.

"I know, to you this seems fast. I'm not into a long engagement. Look, you will like California - sun and surf - just what boys your age love," Tim said trying to make things better.

"Well, I've been to California and it is a great place," Bobby said as he wiped his mouth on his napkin. They talked some more and the boys finally gave up and went to their back room to play games. Bobby went to an old friend's house nearby to visit and probably stay the night. When things got quiet, Tim and Tilly sat in front of the fireplace. Tim retrieved some wood and started a fire.

"The steps look a little sturdier. You must have tried to fix them. I noticed the fig tree is getting big, when the leaves come back on it in the spring it will be huge," Tim said as he kicked the door closed with his arms full of wood. Tilly jumped up to help him.

"I know. I should cut it back in a few months. It kills the grass all around it. I did put some nails in the boards of the steps," Tilly replied.

They sat down together with some coffee. Tim put his arms around Tilly.

"It'll be all right. They'll come around," Tim assured Tilly, knowing she was still worried about her boys.

Tilly spent the next few days in a panic. The wedding was set for the Christmas holidays - December 27 - while the boys were out of school. The ceremony was simple with all of their close church friends and family. It was at the reception that the helicopters were spotted. They had arranged a private helicopter to take them to a remote area, and then take a plane trip to Hawaii. It was hectic trying to dodge the news hounds and everything had to be done secretly. Tim had actually flown Sis up with all her brood and her new boyfriend.

Tilly thought about how much Sis had become like Bonnie. Tilly could see some positive changes coming over Bobby with Tim's counsel. Maybe Tim could help Sis. She hoped for a new beginning for all of them.

Tim and Tilly took off to Hawaii for a few weeks, and Bobby took over the boys for that time. Rae would also be there for the boys. Sis decided to stay a few weeks to visit around. Tilly was glad for her to stay.

The honeymoon was magical to Tilly. It was like living in a dream, and Tim was wonderful.

They arrived at a pink stucco hotel and Tilly noticed the nice details of the building. They walked into an open foyer toward the desk and were welcomed by ladies in Hawaiian dress. The ladies placed leis around their necks and smiled. They were escorted to a simple but elegant room, and Tilly took it all in. Outside the window doves were sitting on the sill. Tim smiled at the sight and winked at Tilly. His smiled faded when Tilly started doing a dance as if in agony. He ran over to her and realized the reason for her torment. It was the lei! It was filled with crawling ants! He snatched it off before he also felt the bites from his own lei. When they had gotten rid of the ants, Tilly sit down and said, "Well, that is my luck, something so beautiful caused such grief."

"Now Tilly, stop it, don't even go there. Let's just have fun. There is a luau tonight, let's go," Tim said pulling Tilly off the bed.

Tilly sat at the luau smelling the strange foods and enjoying the activity around her. She tried the poi and other foods. She even tried to hula, falling into Tim's arms screaming with laughter. They took late night walks along the beach.

The time was too short and they were leaving before they knew it. Tilly was a little sad to be leaving this paradise. She had things to do though, and had to set up house in California. It was decided that the boys would stay a few weeks with Bobby in charge. This was a scary thought for Tilly, but Rae was being a mother to them also when she came home from school. Tilly called them all every day with instructions. The boys would join them later, but Tilly wasn't convinced that this was a good plan, so Tim made arrangements for her to fly home every other weekend. It was hard to raise kids this way and she felt guilty, especially when tongues wagged at church about the children being left.

"You know Bobby can handle the boys, maybe even do a better job right now than bringing them here in the middle of a semester," Tim was saying to Tilly during one of their many discussions about the boys. She was angry with Tim's attitude.

"It has been a month and a half. I have to have them with me. I can't stand it. It is just not right," Tilly said with frustration.

"Why do you have to have them here? Is it because of a few people's opinion, or is it because you really think it would help the boys right now? They will be seventeen in a few months. Look... I have a big trip coming up with this movie. You could go back for a month or two. I'll come visit there," Tim said, and Tilly looked at him with approval. She did not catch the hurt that she had caused Tim. She was right of course, she needed her children and they needed her. Tim had hoped she would join him, but that was unrealistic under the circumstances. This was what he dreaded, the conflict. Had he acted in haste when he insisted on a quick wedding?

Tilly started packing to leave for home. She stood around looking at the house and listened to the silence in it. Tim was gone for the day. The maid was quietly doing her job. Tilly sat down on the bed. What had she been thinking? Tim and she really did not know each other. What was a romance of emails and letters? Would Tim still love her? She was making it difficult for him. Tim was easy to love, but was she? She knew her children's best interests came first, and what happens with this decision happens. Her mind flashed back to the fantasy honeymoon, with Tim buying everything she admired. She had stared at him while he slept. How gentle he had been. He treated her like a princess. He had told her she would not have to work again and the children would have what they needed for college and Rae for medical school. Tilly had little time between the engagement and the wedding to think about everything. Tim walked in on her as she was deep in thought.

"What's the matter?" Tim asked. This startled Tilly.

"I didn't hear you come in. Can I get you some lunch...or something?" Tilly asked. Tim grabbed Tilly and hugged her.

"I...don't know what to think. I...uh...haven't really had time to think about all of this...you know. I guess...I really never thought we would be married. Here I am messing it up. You could have so much more," Tilly whimpered.

"Honey, no...don't. I may have this leading man image and all, but I believe in family. You have to be with them. Did you think you were giving up that part of you? I am more in love with you now because of your commitment to your children. I didn't know how much I loved you til now. I will miss you, but I will come as often as I can and then we will be together soon," Tim said.

"Oh Tim, I love you so much," Tilly said and she held onto him until she had to finish packing.

Chapter 19

Spring 2000

Tilly settled back home for a few weeks. She visited the hospital where she had worked. They had thrown her a surprise shower. They wondered how she had kept the relationship with Tim a secret. Her older African-American friend Ella had pulled her aside and asked her if she was keeping busy. Ella was a flamboyant individual with a laugh that vibrated the walls. She was a large woman with bright gold glasses and a smile that won everyone over. She could always pick up on Tilly's feelings. Ella talked her into coming in and volunteering a couple of days a week. She had sensed Tilly's restlessness. Tilly was thankful to continue her work at the hospital, even if it was for a short time. Tilly had worked so hard on her nursing degree and wanted to use her skills. She felt like she did not fit in anywhere anymore, but the hospital work satisfied her.

One evening when she came home, she found the boys waiting for her in the living room.

"What's up?" Tilly asked putting down some groceries she had picked up on the way home.

"Grandma called. Dad didn't get parole," Hank Jr. said.

Tilly went over to the boys on the couch and hugged them.

"I'm sorry. He did kill someone..." Tilly started to say more but Matt jumped up.

"It was self-defense Mom!" Matt exclaimed.

"I know, but you know your dad's anger. He beat the guy to death. That was not necessary and the courts saw that. He also has a record of violent behavior. He didn't stand a chance of getting out...at least not this soon," Tilly said. She hated that the boys had to go through this.

"Grandma was upset," Hank Jr. said.

"I'll call her," Tilly said.

"Grandma said Dad was going to Chapel every day," Matt said hopefully.

"That is good news. People can change, and maybe he will get out in a couple of years," Tilly assured the boys. They were not happy and left the room. She was put out at Hank's mom for calling and upsetting the boys. She did not care to call them much or invite them to her house, but she could call them with bad news. They had longed for their dad's love. They missed out on this. Sonny always came and got Rae, and Tilly was hurt that the boys did not have at least that. Sonny tried to step in sometimes, but it wasn't the same. She looked over at the groceries and jumped up to put them away.

She was in the kitchen putting things away, thinking about things when she grabbed the milk. She sighed. Susan had been at the milk section in the store, and she had practically run her cart into Tilly's. Susan had mumbled something and quickly got away. Tilly shook her head as she put the milk in the refrigerator. Would things ever change? She had seen some of Susan's cronies in town on and off these past few days and got the same response. Tilly had plenty of friends to make up for the cold shoulders of others, but it still hurt. The phone rang and startled Tilly. She answered and Tim's upbeat voice rang out. She smiled and told him everything. It was nice to have him to lift her burdens.

Tim knew Tilly was volunteering at the hospital and was glad she was happy doing that. He told her she would get a chance to work with him in Africa, and that would be a good place to use her nursing skills in the future. Tilly had actually thought of that possibility, but thought Tim might object. Tilly hung up the phone happy and content, at least for the moment. There was a knock at the door.

"Hey, anybody home?" It was Diane.

"Diane...come on in," Tilly said as she opened the screen. They both hugged and sat down. Diane had a funny look on her face.

"What is the matter Diane?" Tilly finally asked after a lot of small talk.

"It is Susan and her friends...they say you are probably separated from Tim already. They don't care about the truth. Ugly rumors are good to spread," Diane said and bit her lip.

"It's all right, they'll soon see," Tilly said.

"Look...I have done my best to tell everyone the truth, but it does look suspicious. I do understand though...and I think this is the right thing to do," Diane voice dropped.

"You don't sound convinced," Tilly said.

"Well...if I had married Tim Reynolds I would not let him out of my sight," Diane snapped. Tilly slumped back on the couch.

"Tim will be here next week. That will put the fire out of the rumors. Thanks for telling me. Do you want something to eat or drink?" Tilly asked getting up.

"No Sonny will be home soon and I need to cook for him," Diane said looking at her watch and getting up. She hugged Tilly and slipped out. Tilly sat back down and cried. She was so tired. She found herself wishing for Miss June. What would she have said? Tilly knew. She could hear Miss June's voice now, telling her to pray and keep the faith...this too will pass.

Tim arrived in town a few days after Tilly had spoken to Diane. Tilly spilled all this out to Tim as she threw herself into his arms at the airport. She had decided to drive to pick him up. She hated driving around the city of Atlanta, but couldn't wait for Tim to take a limo or a cab home. He would normally have done that to save her the horrendous drive. He was surprised to see her. The look on her face said a lot. She had said so much at once that nothing was making sense until the ride home. He slowly questioned her and was able to decipher what was going on back at home.

"I'm speaking tomorrow...perhaps I could say something to help the situation. Tilly, it won't do any good if you are going to let everything that people say get to you," Tim finally said after listening to Tilly for a few minutes.

"Oh...I know...I'm unsure of things myself and I'm worried about my decision. Maybe we can talk to the boys and move sooner," Tilly said.

"Tilly we have talked about this. I'm not home anyway. You would be alone there too." Tim said.

"I know, but the talk would not be about us around here anymore," Tilly shot back.

"The talk will stop when you let it stop," Tim said as someone cut in front of the car. Tilly did not want to drive back and he took the wheel even though he was very tired. Tim almost did not hit the brakes fast enough.

"Look...Til, as you can see, I'm exhausted and my reflexes aren't very good. Can we not argue?" Tim said and sighed.

"I'm sorry. I did not want to argue. I should have let you take a cab home," Tilly said apologetically.

"Don't worry about it. I was glad to see you," Tim said and took her hand.

"I think you are going to need both your hands in this traffic," Tilly said and they both laughed.

Chapter 20

2000-2001

After putting a few rumors to rest, Tim and Tilly settled into the routine of Tim flying in every other week or so. The boys were doing well with the situation. Bobby left again to live with Sis. He had found a job in Florida and decided that it would be a great place to start over. Tilly couldn't blame him, though she wondered what to do about the house. Rae soon spoke up and wanted the house to come to when she was in town from school. It made sense, and Tilly decided to keep it for her use. They prepared to move for the summer.

Before long they found themselves settling into the house in California. The view was breathtaking and the boys seemed excited, especially looking around at the pretty girls. The beach was so close and they spent a great deal of time there. Tilly thought it was going well. Rae stayed some of the summer before she went back to school. It was a good summer.

The boys were enrolled in the private school Tim had picked out. They were given a BMW because it was safe. They were cooperating so far. Tilly held her breath. The first time they put on the school uniforms, the peace was shattered. They wanted their baggy pants and the friends they had met on the beach, not the ones Tim wanted them to meet.

The first week of school was painful. They hated it. They wanted the atmosphere of public school. Tim argued with them. Tilly just tried to keep the peace.

Tim was gone most of the time, just like he had predicted. Tilly was left to listen to endless complaints from the boys. They did not do their work and they spent too much time surfing. This would not do for their last year of school. It wasn't long before the teachers were calling. It was for small incidents, but Tilly was getting nervous and wondered what they would do next. She knew her boys. The school would not put up with the boys' antics for long. Tilly did not tell Tim about the boys, because she did not want to worry him. He was doing the best he could for them all.

Tim was home on one rare day when the phone rang. He picked it up and got an earful from the school about the boys. They were skipping school and were close to being kicked out. Tim hung up the phone when Tilly came into the room from the kitchen.

"The school? Why didn't you tell me what was going on?" Tim asked.

"What did they say?" Tilly asked timidly.

"Plenty," Tim said angrily.

"What did they do this time?" Tilly asked as she sat down.

"Oh...just that they are now missing in action. Have any idea where they might be?" Tim folded his arms.

"Probably the beach," Tilly said.

"How long have they been getting into trouble?" Tim asked as he sat down heavily next to Tilly.

"A lot. They don't do their homework and they play around at school. I knew they would not fit in," Tilly said as she bit her lower lip. Tim knew she was getting nervous.

"Honey, why do you try to do everything on your own? I'm your husband now. You needed to tell me," he said and hugged her.

"I know...but I did not want anything to come between us. I just thought they would straighten up," she said weeping.

"So you took it on yourself to handle all this. I married you to be your partner too. We need to work together, otherwise they will divide and conquer," Tim said trying to lighten things up, and Tilly smiled.

"Tilly, you know you can't give in to this behavior. They need to understand a few things," Tim said.

"Yeah I know, but the private school scene at this time of their lives is a big adjustment. They are not used to an environment of that kind. You know... they were doing well at home before we left. I thought they would keep it up and get into school more. Change has always thrown them," she said.

"Tilly you are making excuses for them," Tim said and got up to get something to drink.

"I know...I'm just wondering if it would be better for them back at the public school after all," Tilly said hesitantly.

"Oh...so they can get totally out of control," Tim shot back holding his forehead.

"You have a headache. I'm sorry," she said and hugged him.

"No, I'm sorry. Is it so wrong to want the best for you and those you love? I wanted to give you a life of less worry, and a life where you could do things for fun and not have to work so hard...and," Tim was still talking when Tilly pulled away.

"So, I was a charity case...someone to rescue...someone to save and make you feel good about it," Tilly's words cut as she remembered Susan's words a few months ago. Tilly's self doubt poured out. She did not think anyone could love her for herself. She felt peace with Tim, but deep inside there was still a nagging voice that said it would not last. Tim was shaking his head.

"I can't believe you just said that. You know, you have this part of you that you hold back. You won't let go..." Tim was saying as Tilly swung around.

"You're never home, Tim. I don't know you. I love you...I do love you, but I don't know you either. You talk to me about a part I'm holding back...well you hold back a whole lot more. Well I have to think about the boys right now and figure out something..." Tilly suddenly said.

"You just changed the subject. How am I going to help you...us when you jump all over the place," Tim shot back.

"I didn't change the subject. It is still the same one. Me and the boys and you. What to do about everything and us together...it is all the same." Tilly was talking as the door opened and a rowdy bunch of kids came in. In the middle of them were her wayward sons. Tilly rolled her eyes. They had been surfing and probably drinking.

"Well...well...look who showed up. Hello boys, we thought you would be studying hard at school. I didn't know there was a holiday," Tim said and Tilly noticed the veins in his temples swell. She had seen that anger once from Tim and she knew he was mad now. The boys didn't stand a chance. The girls and the other boys were quickly scrambling to get out. They were bumping into each other as they left. Tilly would have thought that amusing at another time.

"We just skipped today. That happens every now and then...to everyone...you know," Hank stammered.

"What happens to everyone? Is there some kind of condition that is going around called "skip day," or something more serious that I should know about? Does it hurt until you get to the beach and then you are all better?" Tim said and Matt laughed. Tim gave him a look that quickly took the grin off his face.

"We were just surfing. It was a good day for it," Matt said. Tim walked closer.

"From the smell of you two...you were also keeping company with a few illegal substances. Go wash up, we'll talk about it later," Tim said sternly.

"He can't tell us what to do." Hank flung down his book bag and looked at his mother.

"Go to your rooms now!" Tilly said loudly and firmly, crossing her arms and waiting for them to go up the steps.

Tilly found Tim in the kitchen later, sitting on the stool at the counter. He was drinking a soda, deep in thought. Tilly hugged him.

"I'm sorry," Tilly said.

"For what?" Tim asked gruffly. Tilly started to walk out. She did not want a fight right now. Tim grabbed her arm and pulled her back.

"Why don't you let go? Why don't you trust me?" Tim asked, and kept a firm grip on her hand even though he could feel her trying to escape. Tilly then crumbled in his arms as if in surrender.

"You know, you were right, we don't know each other. I've been gone a lot...too much. I thought long and hard about marrying again. It is tough being married in this business...and then there are the mission trips. I was hoping you would go with me when the boys get into college...I know it's hard to leave them. I wouldn't leave them on a deserted island right now, they would still find trouble," Tim said and they both laughed. They could always find some humor in everything, and that was what was good about their relationship.

"Uh, we will go and enroll them in the, whatever the name of the school is here, tomorrow. You know that won't solve the problem," Tim declared after some silence between the two. Tilly hugged him again and gave him her winning smile. Tim took in that smile and remembered every reason he loved this woman.

"I'm going to have a talk with them and lay down some rules. I also hope the friends they have met at the church around the corner will help. They've been invited to some of the functions for the teens. The preacher is good and loves young people," Tilly said.

"Do you like that church? I realize I have not made it to church much with this deadline coming up, but I hope I'll have more time soon," Tim said.

"You are right. You have been bad," Tilly laughed teasing Tim.

"I like the sermons, but he is no Preacher James... and it doesn't feel like home," Tilly continued.

"I don't know why you long for home so much...those people with exception of a few...did a number on you," Tim said.

"I know, but you are right, there are a few whom I love and miss. I did live there all my life. There are lots of good people at home and there are lots of bad people at home. That is true of anywhere one lives," Tilly said and Tim agreed.

The boys settled down in the new school, perhaps because they saw a side of Tim that they did not want to see again anytime soon. They also knew that it would be back to another private school if they did not do well.

They had their best interest in mind anyway. Tilly did not care about their motives right now, just that they finished school and got into a college. She did not completely let up knowing that they had their moments of going back to their old ways. She kept a close eye on them.

For the summer break, Tim thought it would be a good idea to go on a mission trip and bring the boys and Rae. Tilly agreed and was excited. The boys, however, grumbled. Rae was ready for a trip, after the break-up with her boyfriend. Tilly thought that they would get back together again, but this would be a good trip right now and the plans were made.

Chapter 21

Summer 2001

They landed in Africa safely and Tilly took in the beauty of the area. They had reached their destination, Nkhata Bay in Malawi. They viewed the lush colors of Lake Malawi, "Lake of a Thousand Shinning Stars." It is the largest fresh water body of water in the world.

When they reached the small apartment-like lodging with a great view of the lake, two men came up grinning and talking fast. Tim exchanged some words with them in Chechewa, the predominant language, even though the official language is English. They turned to Tilly and the children.

"Tilly, this is Sondai and Moyo. They are great friends of mine, converts for many years," Tim said and introduced them to the children too. Tilly exchanged some small talk about the area and Tim asked after their families. He knew Sondai had a sickly wife and promised to visit them before he left. Tilly was impressed with Tim's ability to communicate with these people so easily. She thought about how little she did know him.

They settled quickly into the lodge and took in their surroundings. Tilly was taken with the warm-hearted people. Most could speak

English. They lived up to their name of "Warm Heart of Africa." Tilly read that Malalwi was about 55 percent Protestant, 20 percent Roman Catholic and 20 percent Muslim. The remaining 5 percent belong to traditional African religions.

Tilly was astounded with the bird life in the area. Elephants, hippopotami and crocodiles could be seen in their natural habitats. The orchids and other wild flowers were breathtaking. They hiked and sailed, taking in the rolling hills of Nyika, the forested plateau of Zomba, mountainous Mulanje Massif and the fertile Shire Valley. It was the trip of a lifetime, and good for her children.

Tim led Bible studies with Tilly's help. The boys and Rae taught the children some Bible stories. They were maturing before her eyes. One day when Tilly was standing in front of her lodge watching the boys with some of the children Tim came up behind her grabbing her and hugging her.

"I see the boys are playing ball and making up the rules as they go along," Tim said after kissing Tilly. Tilly smiled.

"They always make up their own rules, but the kids are catching on to their sneaky ways," Tilly said laughing as all the children jumped on Hank Jr. and Matt, hanging onto them and pulling them down.

"This has been good for them," Tilly said laughing.

"Yes, it is good for them to see how others live, and to know how good they have it. A lot of people die of AIDS here and the life expectancy is not long," Tim said sadly.

"You used to bring your children here, didn't you?" Tilly asked remembering some letters pertaining to that.

"Yes, before they got married. It was always good for them to help with the mission," Tim was saying before his friend Gamba came running up, excited and talking in his native tongue. Tim talked with him off to the side for a few minutes and came back to Tilly.

"Tilly, there is some bad news. There is a small village outside Zomba that was burned. The clinic that my children and I helped build was torched. I need to check on it and the people. We don't have the details yet. I'll leave in the morning," Tim said.

"I'm going with you," Tilly stated firmly.

"No, you had best stay here with the kids. This could be the work of a group of terrorists. There has been a recent riot over deportation of some foreign nationals. It could be dangerous because Christians are targeted," Tim said.

"I'm going Tim. I might be needed with my nursing skills. The kids will be fine here won't they?" Tilly asked, now uncertain about everything.

"Yes the kids will be safe, but are you sure about this?" Tim asked. Tilly just nodded.

The boys and Rae were given instructions on a few things before Tilly and Tim set off with Moyo to the village. It took a couple of hours with a few more minutes on a questionable road. The foliage scratched the sides of the jeep and more than once slapped at the occupants inside. They arrived mid-day and it was hot. A man was standing at the road's end and greeted them. It was Dr. Jack.

Dr. Jack, as they called him, volunteered every year here, making the long trip from the United States. He was about Tim's age. He, too, was a Christian, and felt this was his mission field. He grabbed Tim's hand with urgency and met Tilly. He knew Moyo and spoke to him in Chechewa. Dr. Jack let them in on the situation. It seemed that the Chapel also had been burned.

"Is there anything left to work with?" Tim asked as they surveyed the clinic ruins.

"We have some supplies in the small storage unit out back. Look...I'm headed back home tomorrow, and I won't be back for a few months. I don't know what I can do right now," Dr. Jack said as they walked along kicking at some of the burned, unidentified objects around them.

"Yes, you need to go back home...uh there is really nothing we can do until we rebuild," Tim said as he looked around.

Dr. Jack saw Tilly engaged in a conversation with one of the children and pulled Tim aside and talked in a low voice.

"I think it might be dangerous right now," Dr. Jack said glancing at Tilly and Tim looked over at her.

"What terrorist group?" Tim asked, now knowing that the worst might have happened.

"We don't know what group, but we know it was terrorists. They want us out of here," Dr. Jack said still trying to keep the conversation low. "Some of the people are missing. We don't know if they ran or were taken.

"Has there been any trouble in places around here recently?" Tim asked.

"Yes. There have been fires, kidnappings and killings. It has always been safe around here, but not anymore since the terrorist have reached us," Dr. Jack stated.

"I can do some investigation and see what kind of trouble we are in. I'll take Tilly back to the lodge tomorrow and maybe come back. I don't want her in any danger," Tim said taking his baseball hat off and rubbing his hair back. It was hot out today.

"She seems nice," Dr. Jack said about Tilly.

"Yeah, she is the best. Had sort of a rough upbringing and came through it better than most. She doesn't need this right now," Tim said.

Tim talked to Tilly that evening as they settled down on some old cots. She didn't like the idea of going back and having Tim in danger. She decided she would try to talk him out of coming back to this place until they had more information and it was safer. She fell asleep with that on her mind. She awoke to see Tim getting up early. He told her he had heard a noise and would check it out. She waited for him, awake for a while, then fell back asleep. She was awakened again by Moyo at the door of the hut. He was talking incoherently and pointing. She heard shots fired, and jumped out of the cot. Reality hit as she put her boots on and took off running in the direction of the shots. Moyo was behind her yelling.

"No Miss, you stay. Tim say you to stay here with me." Moyo kept following her because she was not stopping. More shots were heard and she ran faster through unknown plants that slapped her legs and face. She heard a snake hiss and jumped. She kept on until she came to a clearing and fell to her knees in exhaustion. She heard a moan and saw her beloved Tim lying in a pool of blood nearby. She crawled over on her hands and knees, not caring about the cuts that she was receiving. She cradled his head in her lap and rubbed his face. He looked up at her and coughed.

"I'm so sorry Tilly...I love you so much..." he gasped, and Tilly felt his life leave his body. She screamed, and Moyo fell down beside her and his scream blended with hers. They both wept and stayed in that position until Dr. Jack found them.

Tilly did not remember the trip home; she was in a daze. Dr. Jack had taken care of all the arrangements in getting Tim's body home and making sure that Tilly was taken care of on the way back. Rae and the boys were silent. They were crushed. They went to the home in California for a few months. Tim's family had been wonderful to her and the kids. Rae had not gone back to school the next semester and stayed with her mom. They needed each other for a time until they began to feel some life again.

Every step Tilly took in the house was painful. Tim was everywhere here. She decided to go home to Atlanta. She felt the need to surround herself with the comfort of familiarity. It was time for a new semester and she wanted Rae back at school. She went home with the children. Tim's family did not want her to go, but she had to. He had left her wealthy, yet she wanted to be back in her little home among the pine trees.

That fall, 2001, America had its worst attack in recent history and the nation mourned. Tilly's hurt and fear came out more during that time. Tilly mourned again for herself and her beloved country.

Tilly sat down on her newly bricked steps. It was February in Georgia. It was a cool day, but not cold. She had just pruned the fig tree and she was tired. She surveyed her handiwork. Tilly felt the hard brick steps under her and felt proud that she had finally fixed the place up. The house looked good and she was content. Rae bounced out of the house through the new etched glass storm door.

"Mom, I can't believe you came back here. You could have gone anywhere in the world," Rae said as she plopped down beside her mom.

"I can still travel. I would like that one day. I can always come back here though and that is important. The boys are happy too," Tilly said and hugged Rae.

"Mom, what did you do to the fig tree?" Rae exclaimed.

"I cut it back. Don't worry it will grow back, probably even bigger and better," Tilly assured Rae.

"It looks like you killed it. It's like us though. We've been cut low and we come back stronger and better," Rae said softly.

"You are right Rae. God makes us stronger and better. We never know why things happen the way they do, but we can grow from the experiences. We need to always seek God's will," Tilly said wiping tears from her eyes.

"Mom, you know I email Dr. Jack all the time. He knows I'm headed to medical school. I feel like I am being called into mission work after I get my degree. I want to help Dr. Jack. I can practice here and help him twice a year in Africa," Rae stated as the phone rang. Rae jumped up to get it, knowing she was giving her mom time to take what she had just said in. Tilly shook her head. This was not a surprise to her. Rae could not have known that Tilly had already prayed this through and had become at peace with this decision.

After a while Tilly walked over to the fig tree and examined it. She didn't see the signs of life on the tree, but she knew they were there. She felt the hard cut-away branches. She remembered Tim's words.

"Because I saw thee under the fig tree you will see greater things than these." Tilly whispered the verse. She had to have faith, faith in God.

.

ISBN 141209737-1